THE
Perfect Catch

Based on the Hallmark Channel Original Movie

Cassidy Carter

ISBN: 978-1-952210-67-9

www.hallmarkpublishing.com

Chapter 1

"**O**RDER UP, JESS!"

The call from the kitchen jolted Jessica Parker from her lovely, distracting daydreams. She tore her gaze from the dessert display that she'd been lazily spinning, where the day's featured sweets made slow, endless rounds—just like Jessica's life had lately. She surveyed the almost empty diner and then found herself glancing outside to see an equally barren sidewalk. She sighed. There weren't even any patrons on their way in.

It was a beautiful spring afternoon. Framed by the plate glass window, Parker Falls, Ohio didn't exactly buzz with activity, either. Sure, it had a certain small-town charm—tree-lined streets, the spinning merry-go-round in the park, the sprinkler just outside making a perfectly timed circuit in its quest to keep the grass picturesquely green—but small-town charm wasn't translating to the rush of business that Wesley's Hometown Diner needed right now, and it certainly wasn't inspiring Jess to do much more than daydream.

Jess shook herself and turned, heading across the floor of the diner. She passed her fellow waitress, Nina, coming from the kitchen with an order balanced on her arm. Jess pushed through the kitchen's swinging door and hustled inside. She scooped two plates up from the pass-through as Cal slid them in, and then frowned at the contents with a look of confusion.

"Blue plate and a hot dog?" Jessica said with a laugh. "Didn't I put in a grilled cheese and a wedge salad, Cal?" There were only a few occupied tables in the whole place. Had she bumbled the order?

Cal, her faithful cook, shrugged and shook his head. "Take one guess."

Suddenly realizing what must have happened to her table's food, Jessica turned and weaved through the diner, bemused. Despite the mere trickle of business and the myriad concerns that were piling up lately with the day-to-day operations of the diner, Jess found herself smiling as she moved through the restaurant, balancing the plates on one arm as she paused to right a tilted old photo on the wall. Just before easing up behind Nina, she flashed an even brighter smile at a customer. Jess saw Nina squinting, paused near a table of customers. The order for Jess's table was balanced precariously on the arm of the other waitress, and Nina was using her free hand to adjust her glasses.

Jessica moved next to Nina and whispered, "Nina, hon. Wrong table." Nina, with a huff, allowed herself to be gently turned ninety degrees toward a different table nearby, where she delivered Jess's pilfered grilled cheese and salad.

"Here ya go," Nina said brightly, though Jess knew that her normally bubbly, blonde friend was putting on most of the cheer—Nina seemed exasperated. Jess's missing order delivered, the two women moved to the counter beside the cash register. Nina huffed and took off the trendy, thick-rimmed glasses she wore, frowning as she tried peering through the lenses.

"Oh my gosh. How embarrassing. I just got a new prescription, and it's driving me nuts," Nina said, looking apologetically at Jess.

Nina had worked for Jess since Jess had taken the diner over. Best friends since cheer squad in middle school, they'd been through a lot worse together than a simple pair of wonky eyeglasses. Jess was grateful that Nina was such a constant in her life. Growing up in Parker Falls, a town named after Jessica's great-great everyone, had sometimes been more of a stumbling block for Jess than a boon.

Besides that, it was good to have someone to talk with every day—Cal, their cook, was in his sixties, and many of their regulars were the type who ate dinner at 3:00 p.m. Now in her thirties, Jess wasn't quite ready to give up girl talk for tips on golf or reminiscing about the good ol' days of Parker Falls, back before they'd gotten cell towers and internet.

Jessica put a reassuring hand on her friend's arm and said, "No worries, Nina. I got your back."

Nina smiled gratefully. Jess glanced at the antique clock on the wall and realized that her son should have come back from school by now. She shuffled the plates in her own hands, suddenly worried. *Single parenting—or is it professional juggling?—at its finest.*

"Hey, can you take these to table six?" she asked. With an apprehensive look, Nina nodded and relieved Jessica of the two plates. Jess pointed, and Nina set off in the general direction of table six. Jess hoped that Nina would make it without incident.

Jess pulled her order pad out of her apron, ignored the numbers she'd previously scribbled on it—the ever-increasing amounts of the diner's utility bills—and jotted down a quick grocery list so she wouldn't forget to stop for milk and eggs on the way home. She was just about to pick up the old-fashioned rotary phone by the register when a customer called from behind her.

"Excuse me, please," a voice said. "But I'm waiting?"

Jessica turned to see Wesley climb up on a stool and settle in at the counter. With his sleeves rolled up and his contrasting T-shirt peeking out from his unbuttoned collar, her son was the epitome of eight-year-old cool. He shuffled off the weight of his wide-strapped backpack and straightened his plaid shirt. She heard the sound of a school bus pulling away outside.

Jessica fawned dramatically. "I am so sorry, sir." She paused and feigned contriteness. "What can I get for you?"

Wesley said, "Double burger with fries, extra pickles, cupcakes, and a mega-gulp soda." His tone was hopeful.

If he ate all that junk, he'd be sick to his stomach. Thankfully, this was one parenting call where she didn't have to be the bad guy. Gratefully, Jessica thanked her late grandfather and passed the buck.

"You know our policy, sir. If it's not on the menu, it's not on the plate," she said.

Wesley hammed up his look of defeat. "But you run the place."

Jessica nodded to a line of photos that hung on the wall, a shrine to the diner's storied past. Among them was a picture of her grandfather, who'd started the diner and given the place its name—and who'd been her son's namesake, as well.

Jessica said, "Sorry. It was always my grandpa's rule, and if it was good enough for him, it's good enough for me."

Wesley rolled his eyes. "Aw, Mom."

Jessica grinned and ruffled his dark hair. She was often struck by how much he resembled his father. Feeling a pang of something she'd rather not dwell too long on, she gave Wesley a kiss as he unzipped his backpack, which rested on the counter, and drew out a schoolbook. He opened the book and began leafing through it to find his place.

Jessica asked, "How was school, honey? Did my graham cracker flashcards help?"

Wesley rummaged in the backpack again, sliding out his lunchbox and opening it. He carefully took out a stack of graham crackers with numbers written on them in white icing. He picked up a simple addition problem and crunched into it.

"Well," Wesley said, wiping icing off of his lips with the back of his hand, "I aced my math test!"

"Yeah? Great job! How about we celebrate with milk and more flashcards?"

At one end of the diner, Jess spotted Nina eyeing the TV. Was she trying to focus on what was airing? Wasn't that something you were supposed to do in order to get used to a new eyeglass prescription—or was the trick to read with them?

Nina called, "Don't look now, Jess, but your ex is on TV again."

Jessica turned from the counter. Her mind briefly flashed to Wesley's dad, but when she looked, a baseball game was playing on the small television that perched on a ledge above the well-worn booths of Wesley's.

Oh. *That* ex.

Jessica tried to keep her voice light as she said, "Chase? I don't think a high school boyfriend qualifies as an ex." *He barely qualified as a boyfriend.* She surprised herself with the hint of bitterness she felt. But the smile on her face stayed firmly in place as she continued. "Wesley's dad is 'ex' enough."

Nina pushed her glasses down the bridge of her nose and stepped closer to the TV. Looking over the top of her new frames, she said, "Look, they're replaying Chase's clip from the seventh game again. It never gets old." Though Nina seemed glued to the dramatic scene that was unfolding and a little zoned out as she gaped at the television, the sympathy was clear in her voice.

The news clip replayed on the diner's TV. Chase Taynor, still as handsome in his thirties as he had been during their senior year of high school, threw a pitch that didn't strike out the batter at the plate but instead resulted in a grand slam home run. Jess hadn't been watching the live game, but when she'd caught the clip on the news the night after the incident, she'd sworn the whole city of Boston had let out a collective moan.

The TV reporter said, "Boston was in mourning last fall after losing the seventh game of the series, with many blaming pitcher Chase Taynor for the defeat. Once a star on the mound, Taynor is now a man without a team, and many are wondering if anyone will pick up his contract with just two weeks before the new season starts."

Jessica studied Chase's serious face, not missing the defeat that flashed across his sharp, striking features. The report cut to a clip of Chase swarmed by media, trying to shield his face. A stunning woman with beautiful, flowing hair hung on his arm, looking more like a luxury accessory than a girlfriend. Jess couldn't help feeling a small pang of jealousy. She hoped it didn't show in her expression.

When she pulled her gaze away from the screen, she found Nina studying her. If Nina noticed Jess's discomfort, she let it slide.

"I feel bad for the guy," Nina said, looking back at the TV.

"Oh, come on," Jess sputtered, hoping that Nina hadn't caught on to her. Jess didn't want to talk about Chase when the diner got too slow to do anything but gossip—and those times were frequent lately. "Must hurt to be taken down a few notches, especially for that ego."

The crowd of press on TV swarmed Chase, shouting his name. A female sports reporter said, "Chase! Just a few questions! Have you gotten over giving up the grand slam in game seven of the series?"

"Yeah," Chase said. "My apologies go out to the fans and my teammates, but I've got a short memory. I'm already thinking about next season." *He was always so cool*, Jess thought. *More like his dad than he would ever admit—a man of few words.*

Cal, who had come out of the kitchen, chuckled as he wiped his hands clean on a bar towel. "Wow," he said, pointing to the news. "Miss Supermodel sure doesn't look too happy."

Supermodel? Was that why the stunner looked so familiar? *Of course. He's a hotshot pro athlete—it'd be stereotypical that he'd have a supermodel girlfriend.*

On TV, Chase and the woman quickened their pace, trying to make it out of the crowd of paparazzi. The reporter who he'd just spoken to was undeterred. She fired off a final query. "Are you worried about contract negotiations?"

Chase stopped, his brow furrowing. This was no easy question, and it seemed like one he didn't have a neatly prepared, glib response for. He paused before he responded, looking directly into the camera. "Hey, not a bit. It's all part of the game."

Jess knew that look. It was the same exact one that had been on his face when he'd told her, *We need to talk. I have to tell you something,* all those years ago. She remembered the conversation well, despite the time that had passed. He'd been itching to escape their small town and go off to the big show, ready to cut ties and leave her behind.

You could have gone with him, something in her whispered. Onscreen, Chase was still struggling to get free of the swarm.

Nina said, "Wow, the media is still really hounding him."

Jess nodded sympathetically. "Yeah, I know."

The crush of people surrounding Chase pressed in. The TV reporter got jostled in the pack and stumbled. Chase caught her with a powerful arm.

The supermodel didn't seem impressed with Chase's chivalry. She looked as if she'd just eaten a slice of lemon pie—minus the sugar.

"Careful there," Chase said to the reporter. The reporter fixed him with a huge, beaming smile. Chase smiled back at the woman as she regained her balance.

Yep, Jess thought, *he definitely still has it.*

"Chase always did love the spotlight," Jess said. Glancing over at her son, she didn't miss how Wes was also glued to the coverage of one of his favorite sports heroes.

"Okay, guys, no more questions." Chase was able, somehow, to exit gracefully from the throng of press.

Nina leered at the screen a little. "He still looks *great.*"

Jessica shook her head, wondering why she was giving old-news Chase Taynor any headspace when she should be worried about the slump in the diner's business. She surveyed the near-empty place.

"Empty restaurant, staff glued to the TV." No one

seemed to hear her except Wes. She smiled at him, pointing to his lunchbox and backpack. "Wesley, hon, let's get that order of milk to go. Come on. Time for baseball practice."

Wesley gathered his things, Jessica tossed off her apron, and the pair of them strolled out of the diner, leaving Cal to watch the rest of the news and Nina still fiddling with her wonky new glasses. Once outside, they headed to their car, which Jess knew had seen better days. Wesley pointed to a colorful sign announcing the upcoming Spring Fling festival.

"Hey, Mom, look! That's a new sign. We should drive around town and see where else they put them up."

Jess narrowed her eyes at him. "That has been up all week."

Wesley said, "Are you sure it's okay for you to leave early?" He looked over his shoulder in the direction of the diner. There could have been a mad afternoon stampede for pie and coffee, and it still wouldn't have convinced Jess that Wes's real concern was for the employees who were holding down the fort while they went to practice.

Jessica shrugged. "Like you said, I own the place."

"Great! How about some laser tag? There's that new place that opened up off the highway."

She shook her head. Not this again. "How about baseball practice and then homework time?"

"But, Mom, I can't practice today."

She opened his car door, and he climbed into the passenger's seat, buckling his seatbelt with a huff.

Jessica said tenderly, "And what is it this time?"

Wesley said, "Batter's elbow?"

She clicked her tongue reproachfully. "I may not know baseball, kiddo, but I know that isn't a thing. Let's go."

Maybe Wes wasn't thrilled about practice because

she wasn't exactly the best coach. She was doing her best, but sports weren't her forte. Chase Taynor may be losing sleep over his future big-league contracts, but all Jessica was worried about was helping Wesley learn how to actually hit a ball.

Chapter 2

*T*HE CRACK OF A BAT hitting a ball echoed through the park. Disappointingly, it wasn't Wesley who had hit that ball—rather, the solid *thwack* had been the triumph of some other kid playing close by. A group of parents watching cheered, and Jess tried to ignore the smiling, eager dads who pressed their faces to the chain link fence and offered tips to the team of children. She also tried to ignore the sign that hung over the field, emblazoned with the name she'd been attempting to push out of her mind ever since that distracting news report.

Chase Taynor Field, my tail end, she thought. He'd barely even set foot back in the town where they'd named a whole public sports park after him, and he'd certainly never looked her up if he had.

Not that she ever thought about that. Nope, not at all.

Jessica stood on the pitcher's mound, preparing. "Are you ready?" she asked Wes.

Wes nodded, and Jess sent a wobbling pitch his way. She waited until the ball neared what she thought was the sweet spot, and then she shouted, "And…swing!"

Wesley swung and missed, big time. Jessica frowned.

Holding up a finger, she signaled for Wes to wait. "Hang on a sec, honey. I think I may need to adjust my technique. Let me see."

She dug her phone out of her pocket and loaded up the mobile coaching app that she'd been studying. She peeked down at her iPhone and then back up at Wesley. He looked as though his patience was about as strong as her coaching.

"Okay, easy does it. So, what you need to do is"—she scrolled down—"choke up on the bat."

Wesley sighed and rolled his eyes. The eye rolling was becoming a major day-to-day occurrence, something that Jess was not a huge fan of.

"Like some kid on the internet?" he muttered.

Jessica, ignoring his attitude, served up another gentle pitch. Wesley swung and missed. There were muffled snickers from the group who practiced near them. The kids in the group had paused in their game to gawk at Jess and Wesley.

One of them faux whispered loudly, "Look, his mom is teaching him!"

The group burst into juvenile laughter.

His face flushed with embarrassment, Wesley said, "I'm gonna go get some water."

He jogged off the field and moped to the water fountain. Jessica gathered up their baseball gear, shot a dirty look at the group—who all quieted almost immediately—and started to haul everything toward the car.

On the way, she spotted Mayor Fletcher walking his dog. The friendly older man changed course slightly and came over to Jess. In his sixties and well-liked around town, he was one of Jess's remaining regulars at the diner. His wife had recently put him on a diet, and he'd sworn to Jess that he would strictly be ordering from the healthiest options on the menu. But he still snuck a sweet treat in after lunch every once in a while. In fact, her baked goods were some of her best sellers lately and something she'd been experimenting with in her ever-growing free time.

"Hey, Jess," Mayor Fletcher said. "How's practice going?"

Jessica squinted over at Wes, who had finished dawdling at the water fountain and was now crouched down at the edge of the field, inspecting the toe of his baseball cleats.

"Truthfully, Mayor, not great," she admitted. "Wesley's team has a big game coming up soon. But he's thinking of quitting baseball for good."

The mayor said, "Well, maybe baseball's just not Wesley's sport."

Jessica sighed. "What other sport is there in this town? Wesley's dad gave him the baseball bug but not the training."

He tutted sympathetically. "And how is Wesley's dad? Davis is off in California, I hear."

Jessica was practiced at not reacting to the mention of Davis's name. It was a small town, and folks were notoriously cavalier about what was off-limits—personal business not being on the short list. Mayor Fletcher wasn't the type to gossip, and Jess fought back the bitter urge to bad-mouth her irresponsible ex, knowing that the mayor was just making conversation.

She could do that, push down the anger—the anger *and* the pang of hurt that still surprised her whenever anyone mentioned Wes's dad.

"That was last month," she replied lightly. "Now his band's in Nevada, I think."

Fletcher shook his head. "I don't know how you do

it, Jess. Will we see you tonight at the Spring Fling planning committee?"

Shoot. She'd forgotten about the meeting. Jessica plastered on her best fake smile and said, "You bet, Mayor. I'll be there."

Fletcher gave her a warm squeeze on the shoulder and ambled off to finish his walk. Jess didn't have the luxury of ambling. She hefted the heavy sports bag, balancing several bats in her arms while simultaneously whistling to get Wesley's attention. Wes jogged up and took the bats from her too-full hands.

"We've got to go, bud. You ready?"

Wes nodded. She saw him glance at the kids behind them, who had resumed their game.

"Yeah," he said. "Mom?"

"Yes?"

"Can we just practice at home from now on?"

Jessica's heart broke a little. "We'll see, bud. We'll see."

Thankfully, she and Wes made it home in good time. As Wes had gotten his homework finished, Jess even had time to whip up some darned good mac and cheese with bacon and peas—a favorite of Wes's since he'd been small.

Wes had brushed his teeth and promised to get into his pajamas at bedtime and not fall asleep in his clothes, and he was currently watching television as Jessica studied herself in the mirror, applying her lip gloss in quick strokes. She called over her shoulder to Wesley and waited for him to appear before she nodded to the hangers dangling from the shower rod next to her.

"I can't decide. Blue dress or black?" Brett was always as polished as new silver, and she didn't want to appear frumpy next to him.

Wesley leaned in the doorway of the bathroom. "You're going with Brett, right?"

Jessica said, "Yes." Wes knew that. She wondered where he was going with this.

Wesley said, "Then *orange*."

Jessica, confused, said, "Orange? But you said it makes me look like a pumpkin."

Wesley smiled innocently and shrugged.

"Honey, stop! Brett's a nice guy." She looked thoughtfully over at her mischievous kid. "Come here." Wes, after a moment of hesitation, shuffled toward her.

"You know I'm not trying to replace your dad, right? I would never do that."

Wes's gaze dropped down to the worn tile, and Jessica pulled him close to her. She kissed the top of his head, marveling at how she barely had to bend over these days to do it. He was growing up so fast. She gave him a big hug. He squeezed back. It had been tough on them in the years since Davis had split, but they always got through—together.

"I love you," she said.

She retreated to get ready, choosing the black dress and fixing up her hair. Just as the grandfather clock in the hallway chimed, there was a knock at the door.

As Jess hustled to the front door, she cautioned Wes. "Be nice. I'm off to the Spring Fling planning meeting." She gave him a smile as she rattled off a final instruction. "Have fun with Bonnie while I'm gone."

Jessica opened the door to see Brett, every dark hair in place, his clothes impeccable, standing on her stoop.

Brett whipped a box of candy out from behind his back.

Jessica said, "Right on time, Brett. You're never a minute early or a minute late." *Or very exciting from minute to minute.* She brushed off the catty thought.

Brett shrugged nonchalantly, but his expression said that he took her comment as a compliment. "Hey, I'm like a clock. And I knew you'd still be getting ready, so I sat out front in my car for the last ten minutes. I didn't want to mess with your routine." He stepped inside and then looked at Wesley. "Wes, ya like magic?"

Jessica shifted uncomfortably. Wes had yet to warm up to Brett, no matter how hard—or awkwardly—Brett tried.

Wesley, none-too-enthusiastically, said, "Sure."

Brett pulled three small cups and a ball from his pocket and arranged them on the entryway table, sliding them around, classic shell-game style.

"You think you know where the ball is, don't you?" Brett asked.

Wesley didn't look impressed, and he didn't answer.

Brett prompted, "But do you? Presto!" Brett waved his hands dramatically over the set of cups.

Wesley pointed to a cup, and Brett lifted it to see the ball. His face went blank.

Brett said, "Wait, I…" Brett rearranged them. Wesley pointed to the right one again.

Brett continued, mystified. "How did you do that?"

Wesley said nothing, and Jessica shot him a reproachful look. There was another knock on the door.

"We should head out. Mrs. Carver is here." She patted Brett on the arm, and he gathered up his magic trick, still looking puzzled.

Jessica grabbed Wesley and kissed him, despite his mischievous smile—the same one he'd worn when trying to get her to dress in pumpkin spice for her evening.

Jessica whispered, "Be good, honey." She mussed up his hair the way she knew bugged him.

They slid by Wesley's babysitter as they left, and Jess made sure that Bonnie had Jess's cell phone number, as well as Brett's, just in case.

As they climbed into Brett's car, Jess said quietly, "Look, it's not personal. Wesley just sees himself as my protector."

Brett didn't respond, and they drove toward the community center in silence.

The mood thawed a bit on the way, and soon Brett was animatedly educating Jess on one of his favorite subjects—accident statistics. Jessica and Brett chatted as Brett led her into the community center, his hand on her back. A working dinner was underway.

"All I'm saying," he said as they passed beneath a Spring Fling sign and into a crowd of other volunteers who were serving food, "is that eating while driving is one of the top three road hazards. When you're an independent insurance broker, you get to know this stuff."

"Wow, that's so interesting." Jessica hoped that her tone didn't say otherwise. She found insurance statistics about as exciting as the overdue invoices from her vendors at the diner. She chastised herself to stop being so negative about Brett. What was up with her? There was no denying that Brett was a nice guy. Sure, she'd never felt that spark with him, but he wasn't unpredictable, not the way that Wes's father had been.

Brett continued. "I could tell you stories—a big rig

driver in Vegas eating a meat loaf sandwich, a grandma popping peppermints in Duluth—stories that would curl your hair."

She shoved him playfully as they headed inside. "I already curled my hair. Haven't you noticed?"

At one side of the room, a craft station had been set up with paint and several piles of Spring Fling decorations and signs. Brett didn't answer her. He frowned at the bustle of activity.

Jessica said, "Sorry, I know it's date night. But this makes us even for that insurance convention."

Brett said, "At least *we* had a Hawaiian theme." But his voice was good-natured. He was always good-natured. Jess liked that about him.

Jessica admitted, "True. You've got me there."

Brett surveyed the gathering. "I've sold insurance to half the folks here." He craned his neck to take a better survey of the room's occupants, pointing surreptitiously to a man nearby. "You don't want to know about that guy's preexisting conditions."

Jessica, laughing, said, "Well, thanks for being here. I couldn't miss this. I'm heading up the Spring Fling auction next week, and we're way behind."

Brett shook his head. "Jessica, you're stretched too thin already. Why not let someone else do it?"

"Well, since no one else stepped up, I guess I'll have to stretch even thinner," Jessica answered.

Brett, who seemed to already be forgetting that he'd asked her something, waved at a couple of people dressed in business attire who were huddled in conversation across the room.

"I should say hi to some folks," he said to Jess. "Spring's prime time to up coverage before tornado and cicada season hits."

Jessica said, "Network away." She couldn't help but feel a pang of disappointment as he eagerly left her side. *So much for date night.* She hadn't been thrilled that this was where they'd be passing their time for the evening, but she'd been looking forward to spending time with Brett.

She recalled another Spring Fling where she'd felt much more excited to plan, decorate, and participate. But that one had been so many years ago it was ancient history. Spring Fling Queen, she thought ruefully. Her Spring Fling King likely didn't even remember her name.

She looked around, debating where she'd be the most help. She'd just decided to go and letter the signs for the game booths when a slick, familiar voice sounded from behind her.

"Well, hello, Jessica."

Jessica turned and saw Charlie. She resisted the urge to hold her nose. His cologne usually announced his arrival before he stepped into a room. Her allergies must have been acting up because she'd not smelled him coming. With his slicked-back hair and dress shirt open at the collar, he appeared more like an old-school, scamming car salesman than a forty-something, successful restaurateur.

She forced a smile. "Good to see you, Charlie."

"You, too, Jessica," Charlie said. "How's business?"

Like you don't know. "Well, it was better before you opened up your new restaurant out by the highway."

Just as smarmy and know-it-all as he always was anytime Jess ran across him, Charlie said, "I always thought Parker Falls needed another restaurant. Ya know, something new. Besides, a little friendly competition just helps everyone raise the bar a little."

Jessica, knowing that her false smile was wavering, tried to extricate herself quickly from the conversation. The longer she stayed, the more likely Charlie was to become an insurance statistic.

"Thanks for the marketing lesson." She began to turn away, but his next words stopped her.

"You could always relocate. Your folks moved to Florida, right? I hear it's sunny there. And from what I hear at the bank, you missed the latest payment on your small-business loan?" Charlie's grin wouldn't have been out of place on a shark.

Jessica bristled. Leave it to Parker Falls to have a blabbermouth working at the bank who was family to the man she was in direct competition with. She made a mental note to go down to the local branch in the morning and speak to the management about discussing a customer's personal information.

She snapped back at Charlie. "Tell your brother hi, and we're doing just fine. My grandpa Wesley opened the diner forty years ago, and I've put my heart and soul into keeping it going. We've still got a few tricks up our sleeves."

"Really? Do tell."

"Taco Wednesday's tomorrow. It's gonna be huge."

Charlie pursed his lips, his expression disbelieving. "Taco Wednesdays? Oooh. Oh-kay." He shook his head and walked off.

At least I got rid of him. Her face burned with embarrassment. Had anyone heard their exchange? Brett was still across the room, likely debating the merits of low-deductible plans.

Passing by, the mayor said, "Shouldn't it be Taco Tuesdays?"

Jess blanched. Oh, right. Tomorrow was *Tuesday*. And Taco Tuesday sounded so much better.

"Yeah," Jess said to no one in particular, "if I hadn't just thought of it now."

Chapter 3

*T*HE NEXT MORNING, AFTER A serious chat with the bank manager and a double latte, Jessica was ready to take on Taco Tuesday—the real Taco Wednesday. Her flub from last night was still a little embarrassing, but she'd been so stressed with running the diner that it was no surprise she didn't even know what day it was.

The main problem with Taco Tuesday was that no one knew about it—aside from Jess, Cal, and Nina, who were now sitting in the empty restaurant, trying to keep from going stir-crazy. The day crept by, and lunch passed without a ravenous crowd descending, vying for Mexican food.

Jess needed something to *do*. She accomplished nothing but wasting time as she sat, worrying, running the conversation—confrontation was a better word—with Charlie over and over in her mind.

Nina said, "Don't worry, boss. It's still early." Jess appreciated the comforting words, but they didn't help the bottom line or the wasted cost of the food she might have to scrap if she didn't get inventive with tonight's themed leftovers.

Jessica slumped, feeling defeated. "Taco night's a bust, brunch buddies bombed, and clearly, our theme nights aren't pulling customers in. So on to plan B. Or is it plan M at this point?"

Jessica was determined not to let Charlie get the best of her. Aside from preserving her grandfather's legacy, Jess was dead set on beating the smug fellow business owner at his patronizing game. "I'll think of something," she said to Nina. There had to be a bright side, a way out, and Jess felt herself gravitating back toward hope. She had to—it was her only choice.

Nina, smiling at her boss, said, "You never give up, do ya?"

"I can't," Jess replied. And it was true. Ever since Wes's dad had left, it had been up to Jessica to shoulder raising her son, running the diner, and all of the many tasks that everyday life required, and she took those responsibilities seriously. Everything she did here in Parker Falls, she did out of love. She wasn't just another franchise out by the highway. She had ties to this place, to this town, to these people, even though it seemed as though they'd forgotten that the diner even existed. Jessica looked at a framed photo on the wall of her grandpa standing beside an old canteen truck. He'd started from next to nothing, and protecting what he'd built was important to her.

Jessica knew Nina needed no explanation. Nina had heard Jess bemoan the construction of Charlie's place before. Jess squared her shoulders and tapped her pen on the fading Formica table in front of her. "It took Grandpa years to save up for this place. The least I can do is give Charlie a fight."

Chase zoomed down the expressway, the midafternoon sun warm on his face, too preoccupied with thoughts of what he was leaving behind in Boston to appreciate the beautiful weather. Too much turmoil. Too much uncertainty. He was laying a little heavy on the gas pedal, but the open country felt good after being cooped up in the city for too long. He pushed his rented sports car just a smidge faster. He was headed home, to a place where nothing was ever up in the air, and nothing ever changed.

Hmm, except that.

Chase sped past a new restaurant, Charlie's Cafe, that sat near the expressway. Several cars turned into its parking lot, but Chase kept driving, knowing that his flashy Mercedes convertible would be out of place among trucks and old cars. He didn't want to draw any unnecessary attention on his first day back. Sure, people would know he had returned to Parker Falls. Even folks who weren't sports fans would know that he was the baseball player from all the newscasts, but he was trying to slide in as quietly as possible so that he could lick his wounds at his parents' house for a short while before he had to brave the public.

Chase zoomed past a huge sign that read: Welcome to Parker Falls. The sign had images of a factory worker, a farmer, a happy kid, and a baseball player who looked a lot like Chase. Above the sign was another, an announcement for the upcoming Spring Fling festival.

Wow, now *that* brought him back. His mind drifted to the memory of a young girl with warm hazel eyes and a million-watt smile...a girl who had once made him feel as though just being with her was a home run.

He wondered if Jessica was still living in Parker Falls. Last he'd been back, she'd been newly married to Davis Idle—a rocker whose idea of athletics was chasing after whatever groupies followed his local band around. Chase had never liked the guy. Still, Chase hadn't reconnected with Jess on that or any of his few subsequent visits. Truthfully, he'd made it a point to not reconnect. He'd slunk in and out of town quickly so he wouldn't run into her. He'd thought it might be awkward, since she'd been married.

Thinking of Jess made him remember their breakup, and that didn't improve his mood. Now he needed something to keep his mind off current problems *and* old flames. More distraction. He tried the radio, but every station was country music. There was a tractor taking up a good portion of the road ahead, and he accelerated further and drove around it, tapping his horn with a wave before swerving back into his lane. Chase had a few minutes before he would arrive at his destination. He made a call on his car's speakerphone.

The line rang and then clicked as the other party answered.

Chase didn't wait to be greeted. "Spencer. How's my favorite agent? You promised me something soon."

"And I'll deliver, buddy. I got feelers out to a dozen teams. But this is going to take some time."

Chase could picture Spencer, thirty and slick, as he took Chase's call at his bustling agency, sports photos on the wall of the sleek, modern office behind him. Chase remembered being impressed by Spencer's office and fancy suits. How glamorous the inner workings of pro baseball had seemed to Chase fifteen years ago. Chase had tried to call earlier this morning, but Spence seemed to be dodging him a little.

Chase drummed his fingers on the steering wheel, accelerating a bit more as he rounded a soft bend in the road. "Spencer, spring training started without me! If a team doesn't make me an offer before the season begins, I'm finished."

Spencer paused. "Look, the memory of game seven still hasn't quite settled down. And when I talk to owners, you have a reputation for risky moves. When you're on top, people forgive some ego and swagger. But lately, your arm isn't what it used to be."

"My arm's fine. It's my ego that's taken a bruising. That Channel 10 news piece was a real hatchet job." Chase hadn't turned his TV on in ages, knowing that the replay of that night was on a near-constant loop on the station. He might have dated and dumped one of their programming execs, but that was no call for such a gleeful vendetta against him. And as for his arm? Well, Spencer wasn't saying anything that Chase himself hadn't worried about constantly for the last six months.

"Look, buddy. Just lay low for a while. Stay out of sight and let me do my magic. Okay?" Spencer sounded concerned, and Chase respected his advice.

He sighed. "Well, I found a good place to lay low while things sort themselves out."

"Great! Gonna hit the beaches of Maui with that gal of yours?"

"She's on a perfume shoot in Paris this week," Chase lied. "But I'm headed home to good old Parker Falls, Ohio. You just get me an offer before I'm toast, okay? My fate's in your hands, bud."

"Ok, pal. I'm on your side, remember?" Spencer's tone was reassuring. "And, fingers crossed, I'll have good news soon. There's still time."

As he tapped a button on his steering wheel to hang up the call, Chase caught the reflection of police lights flashing in his rearview mirror.

"Great. Welcome home," Chase groaned, throwing on his blinker to pull off to the side of the road. He put the Mercedes in park and waited as a police officer slowed to a stop behind him, exited his patrol car, and strolled up to the convertible.

When the officer reached the side of the car, Chase explained, "Sorry, officer, I was on a call. Hands-free, of course."

The police officer, all business as he flipped open his ticket pad, said, "License, please."

Chase handed over his license, and the guy eyed it for the briefest second before looking up and breaking into a wide smile. "Chase Taynor?" he said, chuckling.

Chase prepared for another fan run-in. He'd been hoping to avoid those by coming back home.

"Jake!" the police officer said. "Jake Miller. I was a freshman when you were a senior, remember?"

Chase had no clue, but he played along, relieved to not have to rehash the game-seven debacle with yet another fan. "Right. Yeah, Jake!"

Jake said, "Man, I haven't seen you in, what, fifteen years now? Well, except on TV." The officer lowered his voice conspiratorially. "Sorry about that one pitch."

Chase nodded. So much for escaping the replay in Parker Falls.

Jake looked at Chase, a puzzled expression on his face. "Figured you'd be in spring training by now."

"Yeah, well. I just wanted to come back home and relax a little bit, you know?" Chase was starting to get uncomfortable. If this was a prelude to a ticket, it was just the extra kick in the teeth he didn't want to happen right now.

"Well, good timing," the officer said. "Spring Fling kicks off in a few days."

"Oh? Lucky me."

Jake seemed to hesitate but then forged ahead with the question that nearly everyone Chase had crossed paths with had asked since the night of the flubbed pitch. "Say, Chase, I gotta ask…" Jake paused a moment. "In game seven—"

Chase interrupted as politely as he could. He really wasn't in the mood, but he didn't want to be rude to Jake.

"Jake, weren't you gonna write me a ticket or something?"

"Oh, nah, nah," Jake said. "I'm going to let you off with a warning—for old time's sake. See you around."

Jake handed Chase his license and reverted to law mode, his voice serious. "And keep that speed down." With a wink, the officer started to walk back to his car.

Old time's sake. Spring Fling. Chase couldn't shake the nostalgia. He glanced at the clock, glowing from his dashboard. It was still lunch, more or less.

Chase leaned out the window and shouted back at Jake, "You bet. And thanks. Hey, is there still that old diner in town? Still a good place to get a bite?"

Jake paused at the door to his cruiser. He seemed to know where Chase's thoughts were going. "Yeah, Wesley's. And Jess Parker is running it." With a knowing look, Jake climbed into his patrol car and pulled back out onto the highway. Chase, relieved that he'd escaped a ticket, was definitely feeling hungry.

Ten minutes later, Chase had made it into town and parked outside of Wesley's. It looked exactly as he remembered, down to the tiniest detail: burgundy trim, whitewashed stucco, canvas awnings over the entrance emblazoned with the namesake. What was he hoping for—a hometown reunion to soothe his bruised sense of confidence? With a girl who'd probably forgotten him? That an old high school girlfriend would even still care about him enough to give him that boost? *Sad, Taynor*.

He wouldn't be so insecure if Heather really was on a photo shoot in Paris—instead of dodging his calls like his agent had been. His stomach growled. He'd been on the road for a while, and he knew that his parents wouldn't be back from their bridge club for an hour or two, so, feeling a little apprehensive, he unbuckled his seatbelt and got the courage up to get out.

Chapter 4

*J*ESS WAS FEELING A LITTLE less anxious. Inside, the restaurant was anything but full, with only a sprinkling of early dinner customers, but the jukebox was playing, and it made for a lively atmosphere all the same.

Nina, weaving her way out of the kitchen with what appeared to be the wrong order again, stopped Jess as she cruised by with a coffeepot.

"Jess, since it's so slow, do you mind if I take the afternoon off?" Nina asked.

Jessica couldn't resist ribbing the other woman. "Sure. Just tell me you're not sneaking off to Charlie's to apply for a job."

Nina's expression was horrified. "No, no! I need to get these glasses adjusted. They really are driving me nuts."

"I can imagine." Based on the number of order mix-ups they'd had over the past few days, Jess thought that the diner would probably benefit from Nina's afternoon off, too.

Jess shooed at Nina with her coffeepot. "Go, go. I can cover. Wes will be here in a bit, and he can do his homework and eat dinner here."

Nina started off and then stopped, suddenly remembering the plate in her hand. "Do you mind also giving this omelet to the guy at table nine?" she asked, apologetically, nodding toward the customer. Jess didn't have the heart to tell Nina that she was nodding toward the wrong table. It was a good thing that the local optometrist was only a block or so away and Nina could walk. Jess would be nervous if her friend had planned on driving.

Nina squinted. "He's the—yep, the blurry one?"

Jessica laughed. "I got it, hon."

As Nina headed out, muttering about her useless glasses, Jessica hoisted the Denver omelet in one hand, the coffeepot in the other, and made her way over to deliver the food. She didn't recognize the man sitting there from the back of his bowed head, and as she slowed beside the table, she couldn't see his face. It was blocked by a dessert menu.

"Okay," she said brightly, "here is your omelet."

He lowered the menu. Jessica looked down to see Chase.

She almost dropped the plate.

"Chase?" She stood, stunned, and gaped at him for what seemed like an eternity. There was no explanation for how fast her heart started beating—well, except for the fact that he was even better looking now than he'd been as a teenager and even more so than he'd appeared on TV.

"Jessica!" He seemed to be at a loss, too, his eyes wide. "I…I didn't know you…you still worked here."

Jessica recovered, managing what she hoped was a breezy tone. "And I didn't know you were back in town." Another long moment passed before they both relaxed and then chuckled. Thank goodness Nina wasn't here. Jess didn't need an audience for the awkward exchange.

"How are you?" she asked him.

"I'm good. I'm really good. You?"

"Great!" That was the only word she could pull from her still-shocked brain.

There was another awkward beat. They stared at each other some more. Goodness, he was everything that had attracted her in high school—and then some. She was suddenly self-conscious of her simple jeans and T-shirt, stained apron, and flyaway hair.

"Do you want to have a seat?" he gestured to the empty booth across from him.

Jessica said, "Oh, no. No, no, no, no. The dinner rush will be here any second."

Outside in the parking lot, a loud car alarm went off, making Jess jump slightly. Grateful for the interruption and a chance to catch her breath, she turned to look out the window. "For goodness' sake. Who sets their car alarm in Parker Falls?"

Chase reached for his keys and started to rise out of his seat. "That would be me," he said sheepishly.

As she turned back to Chase, ready to slide his plate in front of him and make her escape, they collided. The Denver omelet she'd been holding careened off its plate right onto Chase. It hit the table and exploded into his lap.

Jessica was instantly mortified. "Oh my gosh. I'm so sorry!"

Chase brushed off omelet, laughing. "It's all good. I'm okay."

"No! Don't touch it! I got it." She whipped a towel from her apron, put her coffeepot down, and began brushing at the food that now decorated the table. "I am *so* sorry."

Welcome back, she thought. *Here's a bunch of gooey*

cheese and eggs in your lap!

"No, please, come on," he protested, using a menu to scoop up piles of eggs. She was so focused on the mess and her own embarrassment that she didn't notice Chase watching her—at first.

"Well, now you kind of have to sit down, right?" His tone had changed. His voice had lowered, and Jess looked up to see that wide, warm smile—another thing that had grown exasperatingly more attractive about him.

"Oh, gosh. Such a mess," she said, grimacing. Ignoring the way Chase regarded her from underneath his lashes, she slid into the booth and swept the last of the omelet catastrophe onto the plate she held, holding the platter up to him. "Would you like some hash browns?"

At least he was still laughing. As she set the plate aside, Chase flipped an empty mug that sat beside Jess right side up and poured her a coffee. "So you're running your grandpa's place now?" he asked her.

Jessica felt the frown forming between her eyebrows. "More like it's running *me*. My folks moved to Florida and left me here to manage the circus."

Chase glanced around. "Well, not much changes around here, huh?"

Jessica bristled inside at his implication. Her life was radically different from the last time he'd strolled out of town toward fame and glory. She said, "Oh yeah? Well, actually, I've got myself a new fella. And he is pretty amazing." She deliberately kept her reference to Wesley vague, waiting to see how Chase reacted. It was a little juvenile, but when would she get another chance to needle him?

Chase looked a little surprised. "Oh really?"

Jessica nodded to a photo on the wall. In it, she embraced Wesley from behind. Wes was smiling—a genuine smile, not his mom-you're-embarrassing-me grimace.

Chase smiled. "Cute kid."

"His name is Wesley. And he's my world." She sipped her coffee as they sat. The awkwardness returned. What in the world could she say to him? It had been fifteen years. They were different people now.

"Want more?" Chase asked.

"Kids?" she asked. *Well, this conversation got personal really quick.* Her brain scrambled a bit at the question.

"Coffee," he corrected, holding up the pot.

Jessica, blanching a bit, said, "Right! No, I'm fine. I'm over-caffeinated as it is. It's called single parenting."

Chase avoided her gaze as he said, "I'm really sorry about you and David."

Jessica narrowed her eyes. Davis and Chase hadn't gotten along much when they were younger, but she doubted that Chase would have forgotten his name. "Davis," she corrected, smirking.

Chase said, "Oh, I'm sorry. Davis."

"Well, it's been almost two years, and Wesley and I are doing fine," she assured him.

Chase nodded seriously, but Jess could still see a spark of amusement in his eyes and the slight lift of one corner of his mouth. *He's always been a little bit of a rabble-rouser.*

"So what brings you back?" she asked. "I can't imagine it's for Spring Fling." *Or for an old fling.*

Chase leaned forward in mock challenge. "Why not? You do remember that I was Spring King, right?"

Jessica felt the flutter again. They'd always had great chemistry. When he'd started being scouted, their relationship had quickly gone downhill. Her reaction when Chase had left Parker Falls to play baseball had been to run straight into the arms of the anti-Chase. Aside from the blessing of her son, the only thing she'd gotten out of *that* relationship had been heartache. And here was a reminder of its origin.

Jess leaned forward as well, mirroring his challenge. "You always loved being treated like royalty."

"And the Spring Queen could always knock me down a couple pegs. Still can, I see." He laughed. "Anyway, I'm just lying low while my job situation sorts itself out." He leaned back in the booth, relaxing.

Jess was relaxing, too, remembering how easy it had been to be around Chase when they'd been together. She reached over and topped off his coffee cup. He picked up the menu again and scanned it.

He's probably not going to order any eggs, Jess thought.

An older couple tiptoed over to their booth, timidly waving. Chase's posture changed immediately. He tensed, looking uncomfortable.

The woman said, "Excuse me, Chase Taynor? Can we get a quick photo?" She waited for a beat before plowing on. "We just wanted to tell you this town still loves you in spite of all the—"

Chase cut her off, lowering his head in what looked like—was that embarrassment? "Hey, thanks. I appreciate it."

Jess couldn't believe that the cocky hotshot who was constantly in the news because of his wild antics was embarrassed at a little hometown fanfare. The woman rushed to Chase's side, stumbling over Jess to get there. She stuttered an apology to Jess before crouching so that her husband could snap a photo. After a moment, and with a quick wave, the older couple moved on.

Chase's smile stayed plastered in place until the two were out of sight. He leaned back in toward Jess, lowering his voice. "You know, I can deal with all the losing. I just can't take all the sympathy."

Jessica pursed her lips. "Well, I *almost* feel sorry for you."

Chase feigned offense. "Almost?"

Jessica wagged a finger at him and said, "Hey, you're a baseball star dating a supermodel. I am sorry, but there is only so much sympathy you get."

"I guess *nothing's* really changed around here, then," Chase said, keeping up the front of being mildly put off. Had he expected things to change? Jess wondered what he'd really hoped to find when he came into the diner.

Jessica shrugged and said, "Yep, Mr. Swenson still paints his house purple. And the fountain in front of city hall still sprays cars that drive by, and, uh"—she smiled teasingly—"and, I guess, I am still right here where you left me."

Chase held up a hand. "Oh, whoa, hold on. I believe it was you who broke up with me, remember?"

Before she could fire back at him, Chase's phone lit up, displaying a picture of a smiling woman on a beach, blowing a kiss. He didn't move to answer it, which made the flutter in Jess's stomach start back up again.

"The girlfriend?" Jessica smiled mischievously, feeling like Wes in one of his more impish moments. "Do you call her 'Heather' or 'Miss Runway'?"

She thought back to the year they had been the Spring Fling King and Queen, and he had called her "Queen Fling" for months. She hoped he hadn't outgrown his habit of teasing. It had always made her laugh.

Chase said, "Clearly you haven't lost your sense of humor." He paused, seeming to remember something himself. "And I hear you're dating Brett Thompson?" At her raised eyebrow, he explained, "My mom keeps me up-to-date on local news, like it or not. If my memory isn't too dusty, he was a nice guy."

Jessica said, "Still is." Chase's call went to voice mail, the notification popping up on his screen. The moment stretched. She wasn't sure what else there was to talk about, but she knew that she wouldn't mind if he stayed a bit longer.

Chase checked his watch. "Umm, I have to go. Mom's expecting me. But you'll be seeing me again soon because you owe me an omelet."

Jessica watched him slide out of the booth and don his jacket, cautioning herself not to blurt out anything too mortifying. As he neared the door, she turned in her seat. "Hey, Chase?"

He stopped, turning back.

"Say hi to your folks," she said. At his nod, she added, "And welcome home."

Chase said, "Well, I'm only here for the week, so…" His eyes grew warmer, and she was half afraid that *he* was about to say something mortifying. "I will. It's good to see you, Jess."

"You, too," she replied. And she meant it, more than she thought she would.

Chase smiled and left, casting a glance back as Cal strolled out from the kitchen.

"What was all that about?" Cal asked.

Jessica shook her head. "Ancient history."

Chapter 5

*T*HE NEXT MORNING, JESS HAD almost shaken off the impact of Chase's visit. She'd hustled through her morning, admittedly taking a few extra minutes on her hair and makeup, checking off the list in her head of all the things she had to accomplish for the day. As she and Wesley went out the front door, she suddenly realized how quiet her son had been throughout breakfast.

Jessica steeled herself to broach the subject, bracing for more of Wesley's eye rolling.

"I know yesterday's practice was rough. But what do they say? If you fall off the horse, what do you do?"

"Sell the horse?"

They both giggled. At least he was laughing. That was something. She knew that baseball reminded Wes of his dad. She also knew that the disappointment he felt at Davis's absence wasn't anything she could take away, try as she might. Jessica swung open the front gate and ushered Wes through it onto the sidewalk.

"Listen, honey, if you don't want to play baseball, you don't have to play baseball. It's okay with me."

Wesley shook his head. "But, Mom, I do want to

play! I'm just not that good."

They faced each other on the sidewalk, and she studied him, looking for the face of her baby in the features of the quickly maturing kid in front of her. She wanted to make things easy for him, but they would have to tough this one out together.

"Well, if you want to get better, you have to practice! And for now, you have me as your coach. So, let's go get better, okay?"

They loaded up their gear, and as she buckled her seatbelt, she ignored the urge to run by the diner to check on how business was going—and to see if Chase had stopped back for another omelet.

The chirping of birds, the buzzing of bees, the distant hum of the train that ran through town—none of these sounds woke Chase from the best sleep he'd had in months. No, he was jolted into consciousness by two things simultaneously—one was pleasant, but the other sounded like a prelude to every grounding that he'd ever known growing up in this house.

The boom of his father bellowing up the stairs made Chase's eyes fly open, but the smile on Chase's face had been brought about by the thought of Jessica Parker's parting words from yesterday. *"Welcome home."* They had sounded much sweeter coming from her than the way that Chase had muttered them on his drive into town.

It was way too early. Chase rolled out of the twin bed in his old room and rotated his stiff shoulder. He shuffled into his clothes and shoes and went downstairs, sticking his head out the front door to see his father standing in the driveway. His mother, Lindy Taynor, still radiant in her late fifties, stood next to Mason. She wore a colorful sweater that hurt Chase's still-squinting eyes.

His father's truck was half off the concrete drive, two wheels in the front yard, clearly having tried to maneuver past Chase's car. Mason jerked a thumb toward the Mercedes, which was parked on the street, partly blocking the driveway. Chase took the hint and ran back inside to grab his keys.

Mason Taynor climbed into his truck and moved it out of the way as much as he could as his son got behind the wheel and started up the sports car. Chase slowly backed his car into the driveway. Mason slowly eased out onto the street.

Chase could hear his parents bickering, his mother walking on the driver's side of his dad's truck.

As Mason parked the truck and climbed out, Lindy said, "Why would you make him repark his car? He was sleeping."

Mason replied gruffly, "It's almost nine in the morning, and he was blocking my truck, Lindy." Chase noticed his mother shoot his father *the look*.

"What?" Mason groused at his wife. "I've got an engine to rebuild down at the shop after breakfast."

Lindy called out to Chase. "Left, honey. Turn left."

Chase, yawning broadly, complied.

Mason, frowning, hung out the driver's side window, bellowing to his son, "Too far! Right!"

"You've got plenty of room, honey!" his mother assured him. Chase's attention ping-ponged left and right. He wasn't sure which parent to listen to as they both waved him back. Another significant look was exchanged, this time his father the looker, and his mother the look*ie*.

Chase couldn't help but laugh. He'd forgotten how entertaining they were. Chase spun the steering wheel.

"Look out!" Mason cried.

Crunch. Chase hit the fence. And if that wasn't a coincidence—that he was about to be in trouble after a swing for the fence—Chase didn't know what was.

Chase sat at the kitchen table with his parents, his father reading the paper as his mother served up breakfast. After a prolonged silence, Chase said, "Sorry about the fence."

Lindy said, "Nonsense. It was an old fence." As she spoke, she kept piling food onto Chase's plate until he pulled it out of her reach.

Mason said, "And a perfectly good one."

More silence. Chase was taken back to being seventeen again. Though Chase had grown up, his father's disapproving stare hadn't aged a bit.

Lindy poured coffee, ignoring the uneasy atmosphere. "Anyway, we're so happy having you home, sweetheart. After all the five-star hotels you put us up in when we visit, it's about time I get to take care of you!"

"Thanks, Mom." Chase dug into his breakfast, lowering his head to avoid having to look at his dad.

Mason cleared his throat, and Chase looked up to see him nodding toward the wall. Chase followed Mason's line of sight to see several dramatic paintings of himself at bat and on the mound, framed and hung in a grouping.

Chase took his dad's meaning. "Hey, Mom, great paintings."

Lindy brightened and said, "I painted that one of you

right off the TV. And that one from a magazine cover."

"They're amazing, Mom. Well done." He appeared a lot more heroic in his mom's paintings than he felt in real life. The silence descended again.

Mason buried himself in the sports page, which gave Lindy the opportunity to drop three more pieces of sausage on his plate. Apparently not satisfied, she added a pancake, too. Mason's paper didn't even flicker.

Lindy sat down and said, "Mason, are you going to take a look at the vacuum today?"

Mason lowered the corner of his paper. "Yes, Lindy. I said I would."

"What's wrong with the vacuum?" Chase asked, not caring about the annoyed look his dad shot him for talking with his mouth full.

Mason, cracking a smile, explained. "One of your mother's paintbrushes got stuck in the rollers."

They all shared a laugh, which seemed to lighten the mood. Chase said, "That vacuum has been around since before I was born. Why don't I just buy you a new one?"

Mason screwed up his face, scoffing. "What? You afraid to get your hands dirty fixing it or something?"

Chase said quietly, "No, I didn't mean it like that. I just figured while I'm here—"

Mason cut him off. "I can fix it down at the shop. It's a perfectly good vacuum." He picked up his steaming mug and sipped his coffee. "Just like our perfectly good fence."

Chase stood up from the table, tamping down his urge to snap back at his father. He didn't want to upset his mom. Instead, he leaned over to give Lindy a kiss on the cheek and said, "Maybe I'll go out for a bit. Look around town a little."

Chase watched as Lindy shot Mason another look, and Mason simply went back to the newspaper.

Jess wasn't as hostile toward the sign emblazoned with Chase's name as she and Wes strolled onto the field. She thought about how easy it had been to talk to Chase, to slip back into that familiar feeling of closeness and comfort. Wes unpacked his gear and, grabbing a bat, jogged out a few paces from Jess. Jess refocused and whipped out her phone, consulting her app. After tucking her phone away, she hoisted a ball and got ready to let loose her first pitch.

"Okay, buddy," she encouraged him. "So, you're going to just keep your eye on the ball, right?"

At Wes's serious nod, she muttered under her breath. "That's what they say? Okay." She let the ball fly, knowing that her clumsy overhand pitch would be a bit wild.

Wesley swung and missed.

Jessica said, "Oh! I'm sorry." She winced. "It was just a little high."

Wes got back into position, raising his arms and hefting the bat.

"Look, I know you're good at this," Jess said. *Better than I am at pitching.* "You just need to concentrate. Let's try one more time."

She tossed out another pitch that bonked Wesley directly in the shoulder. Jessica recoiled as Wes dropped the bat, grabbing for the injured spot. He hopped around, trying to shake off the hit.

"I'm sorry! Sorry, honey! Are you okay?" Jess asked.

"I'm fine." He glared at her. There were no tips in her coaching app on what to do if you thwacked a player with a pitch.

"You sure?" She wanted to run over to him, but the stormy look on his face suggested that motherly smothering wouldn't be very welcome right now.

Clutching his bruised arm, Wesley said in an aggravated tone, "Mom, every time we practice together, I just get worse!"

Jessica took a shaky breath. She knew that part of why Wes wasn't getting better was that she wasn't the best coach. Okay, she was a *bad* coach. App or no app, no matter how hard she tried, she couldn't do everything. It was a jarring realization. She tried to stay positive— she had made a pact with herself not to dwell on the negative in the years since Davis had split—but it was a difficult pact to uphold.

"Oh, buddy. I'm so sorry." She searched for something to say, anything that would comfort him and help her bolster her own flagging spirits. "Well—just—let's take a five-minute break?"

Wesley, skulking away toward the water fountains, said, "Fine."

Jess ripped off her baseball mitt. *Where's a real baseball player when you need one?*

Chase drove into the parking lot, turned off his engine, and sat in his car, staring at Parker Falls Athletics Field. It had certainly improved since the days he'd practiced here—the grass was well-maintained, and the clubhouse looked bigger and freshly painted. His eyes landed on the sign above the entrance: Chase Taynor Field. He dropped his head back against the leather of his headrest. *Great.*

The expectations just kept getting higher. His parents had never mentioned that the field had been renamed.

He'd spent the day driving around Parker Falls, reacquainting himself with all the changes that had happened in the years he'd been gone. Though he'd teased Jess about nothing being different around town, there were a lot of things that he'd noticed just weren't the same. He *had* managed to go all day without being recognized, which had been a relief.

Now, taking a break from his tour, he scrunched down in his seat and checked his messages. Nothing. Nothing from Spencer, and nothing from Heather. After he'd ignored her call at the diner, he'd tried several times to call her back, only to be sent straight to voice mail.

Chase let his mind drift to seeing Jess at the diner. He guessed he'd been hoping that she'd somehow lost her appeal since their breakup. It would have soothed his bruised ego. Petty, but he was starting to get the picture that the person he'd grown into these past few years wasn't the most upstanding of guys anyway. And that realization was gnawing at him more and more. This trip home was supposed to have been an escape, not another headlong leap into old misadventures, but he couldn't keep himself from wanting to see Jess again.

Between worrying about his career, his failing relationship, and the friction with his dad, he didn't need a complication like Jess popping into his life, but the pull was definitely there. Chase rested his head on his steering wheel, feeling overwhelmed. It honked loudly. As if he'd conjured her, across the park, Jessica appeared and noticed Chase. He slunk down farther in his seat.

Jessica squinted. "Chase? Chase!" She waved and then walked over to his car.

Be cool, Taynor.

"Hey!" she said with that million-watt smile on her face. He had been stupid to think that her attractiveness would have waned at all in the years he'd been away. If anything, she was prettier.

Chase faked having just seen her—probably poorly—and gave her a big smile. "Oh, hey. How's it going?"

"Good!" She looked at him slightly askance.

"Good," he responded somewhat dumbly.

"What are you doing here?" There was a small crease between her eyebrows. She eyed him warily.

She thinks you're a stalker. Chase scrambled for an explanation.

I'm checking out my field. No, that sounded arrogant.

Just cruising around town! What? Why? Because he wasn't actually a middle-aged man, but a teenaged boy?

"I'm just, uh, I have a…there's a loose wire underneath my dash here." *Smooth. It's got rental plates, genius. She knows it's not yours.*

Jessica's expression hadn't changed. "Right. Do you need me to call for a tow?"

"No. No, I just fixed it. It's all fixed now."

Jessica, thankfully letting him off the hook he was squirming on, said, "So any news on the job front?"

"It's percolating. It's going to take a few days, though, but it's looking *really* good." Was he getting any better at lying? He didn't think so.

"So in the meantime, you're"—she searched for the words—"hiding out?"

Chase put on his dealing-with-the-press face. "Please. I'm not 'hiding out.' I am 'lying low.'" That didn't sound convincing, even to Chase.

"Besides, I mean, who doesn't like the solitude of a plush sports car with a great stereo system?" As if he were really selling it, he rubbed the leather-encased steering wheel lovingly.

Jessica's eyes narrowed. She'd always had the uncanny ability to see right through him—and his bravado.

"Come on. Out with you. There's someone I want you to meet." She beckoned a young boy over as Chase craned to see over the hood.

"Get out of the car. Come on!" she insisted.

Chase was pretty sure she had just used her mom voice on him—and, again, he was surprised at how attractive he found it. He climbed out of the Mercedes, giving the boy a genuine smile. He recognized the kid from the photo at the diner.

Chase asked, "And who's this big guy?"

Wes skidded to a stop beside his mother. His eyes widened. "I'm Wesley."

Jessica said, "Wes, this is Chase. We went to high school together."

Chase held out a hand. "Nice to meet you."

Jessica nudged Wes, who shook Chase's hand. "Chase is a baseball player, too," she explained to Wes.

Realization dawned. Wesley said, "Wait. You're Chase Taynor? From Boston?"

"Yep, little man. One and the same."

Chase braced for the kid to ask him about that ill-fated pitch, but instead, Wesley was silent with awe. When the boy had recovered, he seemed to need a little more verification than just his mom's introduction.

"*The* Chase Taynor? We're on Chase Taynor Field!" Wes exclaimed.

Chase laughed and found himself grinning wider. It had been a while since anyone had genuinely been impressed by him. Most of the platitudes he heard on a daily basis back in Boston came with strings attached. "Guess they had to call it something, right?"

With another gentle nudge, Jess moved Wes in the direction of the playing field. "All right, buddy. Let's get back to work."

Wesley whispered something to Jessica, eyeing Chase.

"No, honey," she responded to the boy. "I don't think that's such a good idea."

"But, Mom, just ask him," Wesley pleaded.

Chase didn't like the looks of this.

"Sweetie"—her voice had become stern—"I'm sure that he has other commitments."

"But, Mom, you don't know how to pitch. And there's a real pitcher standing right here!"

Jessica sighed. "Wesley would like to know if you could help him with some baseball tips."

"Uh, well, I am kind of busy," Chase stammered.

Jessica said, "See, he's kind of busy."

"But he was just sitting in his car," Wesley whined.

Chase couldn't help but break into a laugh. "Kid's got tenacity, huh?"

Wesley put on a pretty major case of puppy dog eyes. "C'mon. Please!"

Wesley's moxie certainly reminded him of Jess. But as Chase considered Wes's dark hair, comparing it to Jess's shining golden locks, he couldn't help but notice that Wes favored Davis quite a bit. Chase wondered if Jess was reminded of her ex-husband every time she saw her son. He shot a quick glance at Jess's wary face. She looked as if she were bracing for him to say no, as though she were used to being disappointed. Chase felt a sharp, sudden sense of anger toward Wes's absentee dad. He cracked.

"Okay, yeah. I'll do it." He didn't miss how Jess's posture relaxed, how the hands that she'd shoved into her pockets went slack. It felt good knowing that his answer had made that apprehensive look disappear from her face. Her smile returning was a bonus.

She leaned in. "Do you do have any idea what you just agreed to?"

Chase threw up his hands. "The kid gave me no choice!"

"That's true." Laughter bubbled up from her, and Chase found himself chuckling along with her.

"All right," she said, the smile reaching her warm hazel eyes now. "See you tomorrow." She didn't look away immediately, and her eyes remained on his for a second or two longer than normal. He shook his head and turned back toward his car. What had he just gotten himself into?

Chapter 6

THE NEXT MORNING, JESSICA PULLED open the shades in Wesley's room, letting the early morning light spread across the walls, which were decorated with sports posters. She'd noticed a few of them absent from the whole scheme over the past few weeks, and she wasn't quite sure what to make of the fact that the posters he had taken down and stashed in his closet had been gifts from his father.

Jessica said, "Morning, kiddo. How'd ya sleep?"

Wes sat up and yawned. "I dreamed I hit a home run."

Jessica closed her eyes as if she were picturing Wes's victory. "Mmm. Well, dreaming is the first step to doing. Come on, get up. Get up!" She ruffled his hair, toying with the messy locks until he swatted her hands away and rolled out of bed.

Jessica started making the bed, and Wes grabbed a pillow from the floor, pitching in. He'd sprung from under the covers so quickly that Jess knew his anticipation level was high. Normally, she had a hard time prying him from the tangle of blankets unless she was making chocolate chip pancakes. He'd gone to sleep the previous night psyched to be training with Chase.

"Mom, how do you know Chase anyway?" Wes asked as he grabbed a corner of his comforter and pulled it toward his headboard.

Jessica didn't think it wise to tell Wesley that she and Chase had been romantically involved. Instead, she said, "Oh, we were in Spring Fling together. Actually, we were the Spring King and Spring Queen."

Wes scratched at his forehead, which did nothing but further muss his bedhead. "So, it's like you were married?"

"No! It was decided by a town vote." Jessica felt her stomach lurch. Would she and Chase have ended up married? He would never have stayed in Parker Falls for her, and she could never have brought herself to leave town all those years ago.

Wesley said, "So, everyone voted you two should be *together*?" He drew out the word together as if there were something that she was missing.

Jessica did not want to explain to Wes that although she and Chase *had* been together, neither of them had been mature enough to sustain the relationship. Further, she didn't want that little revelation to lead to the fact that his father had been Jess's rebound guy. That was just too much for an eight-year-old, no matter how smart Wes was.

"Ohhh-kay. Enough stalling. It's time for you to get dressed. I'll meet you after school and walk you to practice with Chase." Jess heard the kettle she'd put on the stove start to whistle. She wagged a warning finger at Wes as she scurried toward the door. She was just past the doorjamb when she saw him toss back his covers and vault into his bed.

There was a spring in Wes's step—a bounce, nearly—as Wesley, Chase, and Jessica approached the baseball diamond. Wesley had been on cloud nine since she'd picked him up—signing him out of school a bit early was definitely a contributing factor.

Jess was a bundle of nerves, but she was glad that Wes was happy. Chase seemed to be excited to be on the field as well, taking in a big breath once they hit the lush infield. He hefted a sports bag full of professional gear that he'd brought with him, insisting that Wes use his equipment for practice.

Chase was a pro baseball player, true, but he had a pretty wild reputation. Would Wes be okay if she left them to train? Could Chase handle a kid?

She said, "All right, I don't know how much you know about coaching, but—"

Chase interrupted her. "Okay, hey! I've been on baseball diamonds like this my entire life. And I've had some of the best coaching in the world. I know I can teach Wesley the skills he needs to play this great game."

Jessica pursed her lips. "I hope so."

Chase turned to Wes. "Okay, bud. You ready to knock out a home run or two?"

Wesley nodded, game face on. "Definitely!"

Jessica plowed ahead, voicing the concern that had been running around in her head during the whole drive over. "We should probably start by managing expectations and just teaching the basics."

Chase asked, "Are you just going to be hovering here all day?" His voice carried a little of the haughty attitude that had always managed to rankle her.

Jessica fired back. "Oh, wait. So you can ignore thousands of fans, but I'm a distraction?"

Wes snickered beside Chase. Chase shot Jess a look. She could see the smile barely threatening the corners of his lips. *Ooooh.* He had always loved to get her riled. He'd told her, all those years ago, that she was pretty when she was mad. She stood her ground, lifting her chin in challenge.

Chase shooed at her. "You, go to the stands."

She could almost feel her eyebrows hit her hairline.

"Please," he added, likely out of a strong sense of self-preservation. "Give the kid some space."

Wes was full-on giggling now. Jess took a deep, calming breath. "Fine. I have work to do anyway."

She headed up to the stands, stabbing at Chase with her first two fingers as she walked away, mouthing a silent, "I'm watching you." He returned the gesture, making an exaggerated, incredulous face in return. The silly face diffused her annoyance, but she'd never tell him that.

As she turned away, she couldn't help but grin. She found a bleacher about midway up the stands and sat, taking out a stack of small-business marketing books.

Chase clapped his hands together. "Okay, Wes, let's get started with a warm-up."

Jess got lost in her reading, finding that the ability to sit and focus on the problem of the diner with no distractions was something she'd been missing. She jotted down ideas in a notebook on her lap as she flipped the pages of the book she'd opened on the bleachers beside her. She'd been dying to try out some new menu items, but she needed to consider decent profit margins on anything she might change from the existing menu.

There were other considerations too. Her internet research had yielded suggestions for new table configurations, adding a floor map to help with a seating system if she were ever busy enough to need one, and a dozen other little upgrades that would refresh the diner's interior, if only she had the money.

Jess glanced up every so often and watched as Chase held a timer and had Wesley do calisthenics on the grass—repeating sprints, bends, and push-ups.

"Eighteen, nineteen, twenty!" Chase barked. "Okay, let's do some high knees. Go across. Stay focused."

Wes complied. Jess kept an eye on Wes, starting to fret.

"Come on. Get higher!" Chase urged.

Jessica marked her place in her book and called out from the stands. "And what exactly is happening here?"

Chase said, "We're getting in shape."

Jessica replied carefully. "Okay. He's a kid."

Chase called over his shoulder to Jess, but his comeback was a total brush-off. "Great. Outstanding."

"Okay, Mr. Big Time. He's eight. Not eighteen. And this is Parker Falls, not Beantown."

Chase threw back a response, but he was still focused on his watch. "He's an athlete. From the Greek word, meaning 'to fight for a prize.'"

Jess huffed in annoyance. Another thing she needed to work on—fretting over Wes so much. She'd been, admittedly, overprotective of him since the divorce, but he wasn't a six-year-old anymore. She scrutinized Wes as Chase called to him. Wes had been running the prescribed drills the entire time she and Chase had been bickering.

"Okay, okay, let's stop that," Chase said, waving Wes in. Chase's wrist beeped as he paused the stopwatch. Wes collapsed, laughing, onto the field. Her son was having a blast.

"Now let's see what you got!" Chase boomed at Wes.

Jess took a deep, steadying breath—she seemed to be doing a lot of that these days—and bent her head back to her book.

Over the next hour, Jess was amazed at how Wes took to Chase and vice versa. She actually made heaps of progress on her marketing research, able to relax and focus without worrying about Chase being responsible enough to coach Wes. She felt a wave of pride when Wesley tried his hand at pitching, standing in position on the mound as Chase bent down to dust off home plate.

Chase said, "Okay, one sec, then I wanna see you hurl that ball like a rocket."

As soon as Wes turned his back, Wesley hurled the ball, and Chase got hit in the butt. Jessica couldn't stifle her laugh.

Chase eyed her and wagged a finger at Wes. "That's not funny!"

Rubbing the injured area, Chase jerked his head at Wes, signaling that they should change positions. With Wes now at home plate, Chase slipped on a glove and geared up.

"Okay, you ready for this?" Chase lobbed a slow pitch to Wesley, who swung for it. The bat slipped from his grasp and soared skyward. Chase jogged backward, alarm on his face.

"My bad," Wes called, backing up into the chain link fence. Jess winced. But Chase, who dodged the falling bat, didn't give up, and Wes hung in there, trying his hand at fielding next.

Chase tapped a slow grounder to Wesley, but Wesley dropped his glove as the ball rolled right between his feet. Turning to see where the ball had gotten to, Wesley tripped over his shoelaces.

Jess refrained from rushing the field—she was getting better at that—and stayed in her seat, resigned to clap and cheer. "Shake it off, it's okay!"

The next hit, Wes caught, but the momentum of the ball carried him, once again, to the ground. Jessica dropped her head into her hands.

After two hours, they finally called it quits. Jess had to get to the diner for the dinner shift. As they packed up, Chase put a reassuring hand on Wesley's shoulder.

"It's okay, buddy. Keep your head up. I promise tomorrow will go better."

Wes shrugged off Chase's hand and jogged toward the water fountains, his go-to island of solitude. Jess's heart melted a little at Chase's encouraging words, but she was all too familiar with how promises had turned out for her little family in the none-too-distant past. As they walked off the field, Jess hung back. Chase slowed his stride to stay next to her. She dug out her phone and stared at it so she wouldn't have to look directly at Chase, and she kept her voice soft to avoid sounding like she was ungrateful for his help—and to make sure that Wes didn't overhear her.

"Piece of advice—you don't need to teach Wes to swing for the fences, just to swing," Jessica said.

Chase looked at her from the corner of his eye, his expression a little disapproving. "Let the kid dream a little. There's no harm in getting a few tips from a pro."

"Look, he doesn't need a hero. He just needs a coach."

She felt apprehension creep up at the thought of Wes idolizing Chase too much—Chase, the hotshot who'd eventually leave Parker Falls again like he had in the past—like Davis had.

"Trust me," Chase reassured. "We'll focus on the basics. And you never know. Maybe he'll become a slugger."

Jessica shook her head. "Chase Taynor, always going for the glory."

Chase asked, "And what's wrong with going for glory?" There was a hint of sadness in his voice, and Jess didn't like that. Despite her protests to the contrary, she liked confident Chase, Chase with a little swagger.

Jessica said playfully, "Isn't that what brought you back here?" He responded the way she thought he would to her busting his chops—a grin appeared, and he opened his mouth to snap back with his own good-natured barb.

Laughing, she waved a hand to try to cut him off. "I'm kidding!"

Jess's phone pinged and she checked the notifications to see a new text had come in. She swiped to open it.

Chase asked, "Brett?"

Was that a hint of jealousy she'd heard?

"Yeah. The town's festivities start tonight, and he's my date," she explained. "You headed home?"

"Home, the roadhouse, who knows?"

How dramatic. Poor, lonely Chase Taynor, baseball superstar. Jessica took pity.

"Well, it's probably too quaint for a city guy like you, but why don't you stop by the festival? It's better than hiding out." She couldn't deny that she found the idea of seeing Chase at Spring Fling again appealing.

"I am not hiding out," Chase corrected. "I'm lying low."

"Oh. Right."

Wes jogged over, and she turned toward where they'd parked. She laughed as Chase strutted off toward his own car, equipment bag over his shoulder and swagger in full effect.

Chapter 7

*T*HE DINER WASN'T ANYWHERE NEAR busy when Jess arrived to relieve Nina. Still cheerful following her afternoon with Wes and Chase, Jess started stocking the tables to pass the time until the evening decided if it was going to cough up a dinner crowd. She had packed up several pies intended for the Spring Fling and had moved on to expertly balancing pairs of half-empty ketchup bottles on top of each other when Nina came into the dining room from the kitchen.

Nina wrinkled her nose at Jess's ketchup sculptures. "So now we're hoarding ketchup?"

Jessica shook her head. "*Saving* ketchup. Every little bit counts these days."

Nina bit her lower lip, hesitating before she spoke. "Is this about that notice from the bank?" At Jess's surprised look, Nina rushed on. "Sorry. With my new glasses, I kinda couldn't miss it."

Jessica sighed, reaching out to grab her friend's hand. "It's okay. I know you're just worried. I'm late on the payment for my small-business loan. Who knew our freezer would go out the same time as the fryer?"

Nina grimaced. "Not the best time to mention the refrigerator's making a weird noise?"

"Honestly, Nina, if I don't make the payment soon, the bank's gonna foreclose at the end of this month." She paused and looked around the diner, feeling tears threaten. "But *don't* worry. I'm brainstorming solutions." Nina squeezed Jess's hand. Jess stared hard at the worn linoleum and concentrated on not crying.

"Hey," Nina soothed. "Things'll look up. And I'll put low-energy bulbs in the ladies' room tomorrow, okay?"

Jessica laughed, swiping at her eyes. "Thanks. And I'm gonna do a little promotion tonight. Give us some visibility."

Nina put her hand to the sky as if calling on a higher power. "If your pies don't win any prizes, then I don't trust the judges. You're the queen of the unusual pie. Every time you get creative, you knock it out of the park."

Out of the park. Jess shook her head, feeling a little guilty for trying to convince Chase to water down Wes's baseball dreams. Nina was right—to hit it out of the park, you had to swing for the fences.

Jess said, "Thanks. I tried some recipes I've been squirreling away for a new menu. This one's guava-cherry surprise. What better time to test these out than when we've got nothing else to lose?"

The door to the diner opened with a squeak, and Brett strolled in. His eyes went wide when he spotted the pies.

"Hey, Brett," Jess called.

Brett slid up to the front counter, still eyeing the desserts. "Hey, Jess," he said. Then, with a hopeful lilt, he asked, "What's with all the pies?"

Jessica swung around just as he lifted a hand toward the stack of bakery boxes. "Ah, ah, ah! Hands off. I'm entering these in a contest at Spring Fling tonight. Are you picking me up or just meeting me there at the fairgrounds?"

Brett took a seat at the counter and plunked down some printouts. "Jess, I'd love to go. But I just got word of a rate hike. I've got to recalculate the premiums for all my clients." Jess felt a sinking sense of disappointment. This was the third date he'd flaked on in the past month—and their last official one had been that dreadful insurance convention. She supposed that the Spring Fling meeting counted, but she was a little tired of dates that doubled as work or civic commitments.

Jess tested the temperature of a pie that had been sitting on the counter for the past hour, deeming it cool enough to pack up—the last one for tonight.

"But," he said, "you got yourself a paying customer for the next six hours."

Jessica sighed and slid the pie into a plain brown box. He was still going to spend time with her, even if it meant he was going to be hunched over spreadsheets off and on. And he'd be here when she left to go to the Fling, instead of accompanying her the way they'd planned.

"Thank you," she said, folding the hinged lid over the pie and tucking the side tabs in to close the box. "Now if there were a hundred just like you, we'd be set."

Brett didn't respond. She looked up to see him already buried in work.

The sun had set, and it seemed to Jess that the whole town was at the Fling. The high school band was playing, and the Spring Fling Queen, eighteen and pretty, was waving, making Jess a little nostalgic. She scanned the crowd for Chase.

On a stage draped with glittering curtains, the mayor said, "Welcome to the Forty-Second Annual Spring Fling Festival, a week of food, music, and fun, plus our auction Wednesday night to benefit our local schools. And don't forget dancing under the stars, and games and events all through the week!"

Jessica, with Wesley in tow, skirted the crowd that was gathered around Mayor Fletcher and dropped off several pies at a table marked "Contest Entries".

"Okay, honey," she said to Wes, grabbing his hand, "all signed, sealed, and delivered. A blue ribbon or two sure wouldn't hurt business."

Wesley tugged her toward the carnival games set up to the left of the stage. "Your pies are great, Mom. When I bring a slice to school, I'm the most popular kid there."

"Then fingers crossed some of the judges are eight-year-olds."

Wes grinned at her over his shoulder. It was a genuine smile, not one of his mischievous ones, or—as had been the case too often lately—one of his forced ones. In fact, he'd been in a great mood all day. While Wes handed some of his saved allowance money to the barker running the ring toss booth, Jess scanned the room again. Nearby, so close that she was surprised she hadn't spotted them before, stood Chase, Mason, and Lindy. Chase had his coat collar up, trying to look inconspicuous, and his generic baseball cap was pulled down low. Jess held back a snicker. *Not hiding out? Yeah. Right.*

Chase looked like someone was forcing him to floss with barbed wire as Lindy said, "Isn't this great? It's all so much fun. It gets better every year."

"Terrific," Chase agreed. "Well, let's head home."

Lindy thwapped him gently on the arm. "But, honey, we just got here."

Mason cut his eyes at Chase. Jess could see that the look wasn't an amused one. "What's wrong? Disappointed that there's no ticker-tape parade?"

Chase's dad was being a little rough on him.

Jess heard Lindy say, "C'mon, dear, they're displaying some of my paintings in the art tent."

As Lindy and Mason walked off, Jess started to move toward Chase, but a passerby rushed into her path. The woman grabbed Chase's arm, loud and effusive as she clung to him.

"Chase! How ya doing? I just want to say what huge fans we are! And, about what happened—"

Chase cut her off with that fake smile that Jess had seen him put on during the news clip. He clasped the woman's shoulders in a friendly gesture, releasing her quickly and backing into the stream of people between him and Jess. "Oh, hey. Thank you so much. Good to see you," he said. Did he even know the woman, or was the stream of fumbled words just the product of sudden panic?

He turned from the woman's befuddled smile—right around to face Wes and Jessica.

"Oooh," Jess said in mock amazement. "You are very brave for showing up. So you found time in your schedule?"

Chase looked back over his shoulder. The woman had blended back into the crowd. "Someone suggested I shouldn't hide out," he said wryly.

"So why are you hiding under that cap? May I?" She removed his cap and handed it back to him. After a second's study, she ran her fingers through his hair to smooth it. Aside from a few grays here and there, it was the same floppy puppy hair that she'd always teased him about.

"This is just ridiculous," she muttered as she folded down the upturned collar of his coat. Chase closed his eyes, a pained expression on his face.

"Much better," she said, surveying her work. Wes nodded in agreement.

On stage, the mayor said, "And I saved the best for last—when we wrap up the week with the father-son baseball game at Chase Taynor Park." The mayor boomed out over the crowd. "Speaking of whom, did I see Chase Taynor himself out there?"

The crowd had somehow surrounded them, and Jess stepped aside to reveal an embarrassed Chase. People started to cheer at the mention of his name.

"Chase," Mayor Fletcher exclaimed. "Come on up!"

Jessica clapped along with the crowd. "Your public awaits," she prodded him.

Chase flashed her a wan smile. "I was afraid of this."

"Don't be. Just remember to smile." She wanted to tell him to make it a *real* smile.

Chase reluctantly strode up to the stage, and it was obvious that he was a bit uncomfortable at the mic. Jess couldn't, for the life of her, imagine why. Where was that on-camera braggadocio, the confidence of the brash tabloid darling?

The mayor shook Chase's hand. "Chase Taynor, ladies and gentlemen!"

Chase leaned into the mic. "Hey, everybody."

The crowd applauded. Jess and Wes hooted and hollered to increase the crowd's volume.

"It's fantastic to be back home again." Chase looked out over the crowd. He seemed to freeze for a moment, and his gaze dropped. He didn't say anything else. Jess followed his previous line of sight to see that Lindy and Mason had returned. Mason Taynor's stone face was a stark contrast to his wife's beaming smile. Silence stretched.

The mayor leaned in, grabbed the mic, and said, "Well, it's great having you here. And about that game seven... well, who doesn't make a mistake once in a while? But to us, you're still—"

Chase cut in, grabbing the microphone. "I'm not a very good public speaker, but I hope everyone enjoys this year's Spring Fling. Should be the best one ever."

Jess's attention whipped between Chase and Mason. Chase had forced his focus back up and was staring right at his father. Mason crossed his arms over his chest, his expression unwavering.

Chase's trademark confidence began to wobble, and it showed on his face. He looked away from Mason, and his eyes locked on Jess. She mouthed, *"Smile."*

Chase smiled. "It's really good to be back home. Thanks, everyone."

"Give it up for Chase Taynor!" Mayor Fletcher cheered. As people joined in with their own cheers, Chase slipped off the stage, and Jess lost sight of him.

Chase made a beeline back to Jessica and Wesley. When he found them by a table loaded down with baked goods, Wes gave him a fist bump and then an unexpected hug, throwing his arms tight around Chase's middle. Chase lifted a hand, hesitated, and then passed a palm over Wes's neck, squeezing the boy's back.

"Well, that was a train wreck," Chase huffed.

"I thought it was sweet. That's the thing about this town—you stumble; it catches you." As she said it, Chase realized that she actually meant it. He nodded, not fully there yet. Jess certainly didn't have the same opinion of Parker Falls that Chase had. He hated dodging the concerned, caring faces of its citizens. He'd come here to escape the constant reminders of his failures in Boston, not to be *comforted* about them. It was hard pretending confidence, hiding how he was really feeling in a place that had known him since childhood.

Chase inspected the table, noticing Jess's pie entries. "And what's going on here?"

Jessica said, "Just trying to win some visibility and a blue ribbon or two. Things have been slow at the diner."

Guess the Parker Falls hometown safety net only extends so far. He kept his sarcasm to himself. Instead, he asked, "And where's the boyfriend tonight?"

"Brett's working." She quickly changed the subject. "And when do we get to meet the amazing Heather?"

It was Chase who was now on the defensive. "Her shoot wraps tomorrow. She's thinking of flying out here." He searched for anything else to talk about, to move the focus away from the fact that he still hadn't talked to Heather since arriving here.

He smiled at Wesley. "Hey, Wes, how's the arm?"

Wesley said, "Sore from those push-ups."

Chase socked Wes softly in the shoulder. "That's called getting in shape."

Wes winced and managed a weak grin. "Mom, can I go play some more games? My friends are over there." He pointed to a group of kids about his age who were gathered near the pick-a-duck booth. A nearby parent waved to Jess and Chase.

"Sure, honey," Jess said. Wes took off.

Jessica turned back to Chase. He got the same feeling that he'd gotten at the ballpark—that Jess's overprotective side was about to resurface. And he was right.

"Look, Chase," she started, "it's nice you agreed to coach Wes, but maybe this wasn't such a good idea. It didn't exactly go so well."

He stared at her in disbelief. Coaching Wes had been the most fun he'd had since being back. On the field, Chase had forgotten about his parents, about Heather, and about Boston. "Are you giving me the hook?"

Jessica fussed with his jacket collar again. "I'm giving you a chance to get off the hook."

Chase brushed her fidgeting hands down and enveloped both of them in his own. "Hey, I made a promise. And a deal's a deal. Right?" She didn't reply, but she didn't pull away from him, either. "I don't give up that easy," he said. "Looks like you're stuck with me for the week."

Jess nodded, but Chase could tell she was still uneasy. Under his own, her hands were soft and warm. He took what he knew to be longer than he needed to let go of them.

Chapter 8

*I*N THE NEARLY EMPTY DINER the next day, Nina searched for something to clean as Jessica eyed a restaurant magazine, flipping open the glossy volume to an article on food trucks.

She waved the magazine at Nina. "My grandfather started selling sandwiches from his canteen truck to save up for this place, and now food trucks are all the rage. He was ahead of his time."

Nina took a peek. "You're not seriously thinking about getting one, are you?"

"I just think a rolling diner would raise our visibility around town."

Nina's reaction said it all—even her friend had doubts. Jess closed her eyes and nodded in acquiescence to Nina's unspoken point. "Yeah. It's probably not the best idea to take out a second loan when I can't pay off the first one." She closed the magazine, letting it fall onto the counter with a *thwack*.

Nina, polishing a bakery case, stopped and turned to regard Jessica at the noise. Jess assumed that Nina was trying to distract Jess from her money worries when she said, "So I heard that someone's got a new private coach."

Nina pursed her lips in Jess's direction, waiting for some juicy gossip to follow.

Jess rolled her eyes. "You 'heard,' huh?"

Nina said, "Just, you know, word on the street."

"With Wesley's coach retiring and my lack of skill, Chase is pretty much the only alternative," Jess explained. Why did knowing that Parker Falls was talking about her and Chase make her so nervous?

Nina, who had probably been dying to ask Jess her next question all morning, jumped right in. "So, are there any fireworks left from high school?"

Maybe. Jessica recalled the way he'd taken her hands in his, and the serious tone of his voice when he'd said he didn't give up easily. She got that fluttery feeling in her stomach all over again.

But she shook her head. "Uh-uh-uh! This is just a pit stop for Chase on the way back to the big time. It is sensible to keep my distance."

"Since when is sensible any fun?" Nina challenged.

Jessica shot back, "Chase skipped town and never looked back, and Davis left to 'find' himself. At this point, I'll take sensible any day." And it certainly wasn't fair to Brett for Jess to be dishing on an old boyfriend.

Jess stopped at the sight of Nina's raised eyebrow. Jess had probably been a bit more vehement than she'd intended, but it was true—Chase had left before, lighting out without saying goodbye to her. He was leaving again, and that was certain. She wouldn't make the same mistake twice—three times if you counted Davis.

The diner's door popped open, and Brett strolled in. Nina said, "Well, speaking of sensible…right on schedule."

Jess cut her eyes at Nina. "Exactly," she hissed. Once,

Nina had said that she could tell what day it was by the pair of shoes Brett wore. That wasn't a bad thing, in Jess's opinion. Steady. Predictable—except lately, when it came to spending time with Jess.

Jessica said, "Hey, Brett."

"Hi," he said, nodding to Nina as he sauntered up to the counter, his hands in his pockets. He fixed his gaze on Jess. "So how's it working out with Chase coaching Wesley?"

A little taken aback by the abruptness of the question, she shook her head. "Like an ant trying to climb Everest."

Brett blanched. "Aww, poor Wes. He'll figure it out."

Jessica said, "Actually, I was talking about Chase."

Brett laughed. "Well, cheer up. A little something for you, my dear." Brett took an envelope from his jacket pocket. "An invitation."

"To what?" Jessica asked.

He handed her the envelope across the counter. "Our reservation at Le Spectre." He watched her expectantly, waiting for her reaction.

She opened the envelope to find a printout of a beautiful waterfront restaurant. "For my birthday?" Maybe there was hope for them yet. "I can always count on you to remember everything."

Brett tapped his head. "Steel trap."

Behind him, Nina pointed toward Brett's shoes, a pair of loafers that were polished to a shine. She mouthed, *"Tuesday."* As Brett sat down at the counter, Jess felt her smile slipping just the barest fraction.

Chase pulled into the parking lot of Chase Taynor Field and turned his car off. He didn't see any sign of Jess and Wesley, so he hiked to an empty dugout, took out his phone, braced himself, and then made a call. As soon as he heard the familiar voice greet him on the other end, he put up his best upbeat smokescreen. "Spence, tell me good news!"

Spencer said, "You bet, big guy. We got movement."

Chase couldn't keep the hope out of his voice. "Movement? Well, that's great!"

"Well, more like trial balloons," Spencer corrected himself, causing Chase to frown. "But you know how these things go. Any of the real offers wait till the eleventh hour. Listen, I just need you to be patient a little bit longer."

Chase was dispirited. He swallowed down his rising panic. "I'll try."

"I'll talk to you soon." The soft, sudden dead air on the other end let Chase know that Spencer had hung up—and quick. Chase's phone pinged and he looked, hoping the text would be from Spencer, giving him more detail on the interested team. It was Jess. She and Wes should have been here by now. It was way past time for Wes's school to be out and then some.

Sorry we're late. Just parking now.

Chase sighed, put on his game face, and stood up from the player's bench. A moment later, he joined Wesley on the mound. Shaking off his worries and focusing on the tasks ahead of them, Chase gave Wes a few position pointers and then sent him jogging toward home plate. Jessica watched from the stands as Wesley stood at bat.

Chase said to Wesley, "It's the bottom of the ninth. Bases loaded. And here comes the pitch."

Chase tossed an easy pitch. Wesley swung big and

missed. *If only he'd been the one at bat back in Boston.* Chase took in Wes's determined face, and said, "Okay, good power, but meet the ball as it comes in, and you're going to knock it to Mars!"

"If you say so," Wesley said.

Chase flipped another smooth pitch toward Wes. Wes swung, and the bat made light contact with the ball, which bounced off to one side.

"Okay!" Chase cheered. "All right! We'll get it." He was thrilled that Wes had connected with the ball. He was gearing up for his next throw, finding himself forgetting about the phone call, when Jess made a soft "psssst" from behind the fence.

"Hey! Chase! I don't know that your approach is working," she whispered.

Chase forced a smile and tapped his ungloved hand over his mitt. "Time out," he called to Wesley.

Chase looked over at the chain link fence and shot an annoyed glare at Jessica. "Do I come down to the diner and tell you how to bake pies?"

Jessica called out to Wesley. "It's okay, honey! Chin up."

Chase, frustrated, strode toward the stands. "Obviously," he said as he neared Jess, "Wes can't concentrate with all of your helicopter parenting, okay?"

Jessica's eyes sparked. "'Helicopter parenting'? No, I'm sorry, it's called taking an interest in your child."

Chase tossed his glove to the ground. He rubbed his shoulder, wincing.

Jessica said, "Problem?" By the sharp edge in her voice, Chase could tell she wasn't really concerned either way—she was really wondering if *they* had a problem.

Chase took a deep breath. "Just a little stiff. Look, just give us some space and let me do this my way. I'll bring Wesley back to the diner in an hour or so. Okay?"

"Are you okay with that?" Jess asked, tilting her head to see around Chase and address Wesley.

Wesley said, "Yes!" Chase got the idea that Wes wanted a little space, too.

Jessica seemed to think it over. After a tense moment where Chase was afraid she might call the whole thing off, she relented. "Okay. Fine. I have an errand to run anyway."

"Bye." Chase waved. Wesley gave a little wave of his own.

Jess's exit was a little reluctant, and she glanced back a few times as she walked toward the parking lot, but at least she was trusting him with Wes.

Turning back to the field, Chase clapped a few times, loudly. "Great, buddy. Let's try again."

Jessica, still feeling a little guilty for snapping at Chase and nervous because she'd left Wes at the ballpark, strolled past rows of used cars, pausing at the back of the lot where several preowned vans and trucks were parked. She spotted what she'd come to look at—a vehicle that clearly used to be some sort of food truck—big, boxy, and run-down. The pop-out panel on one side appeared to be sealed shut by layers of grime. She studied it. It wasn't the fanciest, shiniest thing, but something about it reminded her of her grandfather's old canteen truck— maybe it was the hood, the sole panel on the thing that had been painted red for some reason.

A salesman approached, jogging enthusiastically out

of the sales office. "Hello there, young lady! Got your eye on a used car?"

Put off by his over-the-top exuberance, Jessica said, "Uh, hi. I'm just looking."

The salesman, slick, even if a little bumbling, said, "Looking's the first step to buying."

"Yeah, not today. But that truck is kind of interesting." She pointed to the junk heap in question.

The salesman nodded. "Don't see food trucks like that baby anymore."

Jessica was careful not to show the level of her interest. She'd gotten pretty good at her poker face since her divorce. It came in handy with vendors at the diner, Wes's teachers, and anywhere else she had to appear tougher and act cooler than she felt. "Looks like it's seen better days."

The salesman eyeballed her haughtily. His tone was a tad patronizing when he replied, "Well, she's a classic. Which is why a truck like this doesn't come cheap." He wagged a finger at Jess, drawing a pen and notepad from his shirt pocket. "Tell you what. I can do something for you, and I think it's really going to help you out. What do you say about that?" He scribbled on the notepad and flashed an offer to Jess.

She looked over tentatively and peeked at the paper. Her eyes widened at the price he had written. "Not in this lifetime."

Disappointed, she stuffed her hands into her pockets and turned away. She had to get back to the diner before the dinner rush, and Chase would be dropping Wes off soon.

The salesman shouted after her, "You know where I am!"

Chase had definitely noticed how much Wes relaxed after his mom made her exit. Leaving Wes had to have been hard for Jess, but Chase truly believed that they could accomplish more without her in the stands. Chase had no doubt that it was tough being a single mom—but it certainly had to be just as tough being an eight-year-old who felt like he had to never, ever disappoint that mom. Chase had, between bouts of drills, praised Wes for being so responsible that his mom would leave him to practice without her. He'd even tapped out a text to Jess to thank her for doing so.

She'd surprised him by texting back a smiley face and a heart. His own heart had squeezed a little in his chest.

Now, trying to focus on Wes and not think about Jessica—and succeeding, mostly—Chase aimed the ball at Wes's ready form. Chase pitched. Wes swung and missed.

"That's okay," Chase reassured the boy. "One more time. Keep your head down, shoulders back, and keep your eye on the ball."

Chase pitched again. Wesley fouled the ball.

Chase felt his shoulders slump. "Let's take five."

Wesley tapped his bat on home plate. Chase could tell the boy was as frustrated as Chase was.

Wesley threw back his head. "This is hopeless. We've been here two hours! I could practice a million years. I'm never gonna be like you."

Wes looked up at Chase, and the emotion on his face made Chase think of the last few days with his own father. No matter how hard Chase tried, there was always the worry that he would never be good enough. It was a hard notion to swallow in his thirties. He couldn't imagine feeling that way at eight.

"Be like me? I don't think that's such a good idea."

Wesley said, "But you're a big star."

"Big star?" Chase scoffed and then shook his head. "Wes, I'm the guy who gave up a grand slam to lose the biggest game of the year. And now, well, my arm's starting to fade, and no team will touch me."

Wes gawked at him, surprised at the confession.

Chase sighed. "Look, my best years might be behind me, but I've got an eye for talent, okay? And I know you have potential. I wouldn't kid about that." He paused to think. "Let's clean up. Let's get you back home."

Chase went to pick up the gear bag, racking his brain for any way he could change up their routine, anything new he could try to help Wes improve. As he turned back toward the field to start gathering the extra bats from the ground, he saw Wesley bend down and scoop up a base-ball. Chase didn't pay much attention to the move until the crack of the bat hitting the ball—a perfect, ringing *crack!* that signified a solid hit—sounded. Wes must have tossed the ball up himself and hit it. Chase's head jerked up in time to see the ball soar into the outfield.

Chase just stared at the boy, a bit flabbergasted.

Wes's stunned face split into a slow, surprised grin.

"Can you do that again?" Chase asked.

It was getting late. Jess resisted the urge to check her phone for the millionth time, knowing that Chase's last text—a simple, *we'll be here for a while longer if that's okay*—should have been good enough to make her not worry. Especially after she'd given permission. But she still couldn't deny that she was overly relieved when Chase and Wesley came striding into the diner, chattering happily.

"I think you're ready for the majors, man," she heard Chase say to Wes, whose face didn't look at all like the defeated one he'd worn when she'd left the field this afternoon.

She came around the counter to meet them, smiling. "What are you so happy about? You two look like some cats that ate some canaries."

Wesley, bursting at the seams, said, "Two base hits, and Chase even taught me some fancy pitches!"

"What? That's great! High five!" She didn't care how nerdy she looked. She smashed a serious high five with her son. "Go clean up, and I'll make you some food."

Wesley marched off, leaving Chase and Jessica on their own. She spun around to face Chase, not even trying to hide her surprise. In a few days, he'd managed to accomplish what Jess hadn't been able to make happen in weeks. Clearly, asking for Chase's help hadn't been such a bad idea.

Looking much lighter, his mood better than when they'd parted, Chase said, "Kid's a natural. Things went surprisingly well."

Jessica couldn't ignore how magnetic he was, even with his hair mussed from being on the field all afternoon and his T-shirt smudged with red clay. Actually, the fact that he'd spent his afternoon helping Wes made him *more* appealing. She tamped down the thought. "How did you do it?"

Chase's expression was mystified. He hesitated for a

second before saying, "I don't know. I just opened up to him about my situation, and he began to improve."

Jessica frowned. "Your situation?"

"You know when you asked me if I had a problem before you left the field?"

She nodded.

"Look, this 'bidding war' is a front. It feels more like an empty battlefield. My arm is just not the same as it used to be," he said softly.

She could tell it hadn't been an easy admission for him. "Hmm, well, maybe admitting you lost was the best way to win him over."

Chase said, "I don't follow."

"Every hero Wesley's ever had disappointed him, especially his dad. All the big promises Davis made— ya know, taking him to a doubleheader in Cleveland, teaching him electric guitar." She paused, shaking her head. "What Wesley needs is somebody who can be real with him. He trusts that."

Their gazes locked. She didn't look away. The impact of those mesmerizing blue eyes hadn't faded at all.

"Well, at least he has you. You give him something real," Chase said.

Jess had to swallow past a sudden burn in her throat. "Thanks," she whispered.

Chase took a step closer to her, and she didn't move. She waited to see if another step would follow.

Wesley burst back into the dining room, and Jess did take that step back. Chase's eyes were still locked onto hers for a split second, but he recovered quickly, blinking and then looking away.

"Chase!" Wes said. "Can you come to my big game tomorrow?"

Jessica could feel her cheeks flush. She turned to her

son. "Sweetie, we've already asked enough of Chase."

Chase cut in. "Honestly, I'm kind of a bad luck charm right now, but if you want me there, I'll be there, buddy."

"Awesome!" Wes did a celebratory dance and zoomed off to the kitchen.

Jess burst out laughing. She turned back to Chase, whose eyes were now soft and amused. She decided right then that she was going to do something that was probably way too intimate and definitely unwise, at least in the complications-with-an-ex department. She was going to ask Chase to come and sit in the kitchen with them while she made some dinner.

"So, Chase—"

The creak of the worn door sounded, and Brett walked in. *Dang.* She'd forgotten that she had invited him over to her house for dinner. And—she glanced at the diner's clock—Brett was right on time.

Brett brushed past Chase as if he wasn't even there and gave Jessica a kiss on the cheek. "Hi babe," he said. "Guess who I just sold a term-life policy to?"

Jessica was taken aback by his rudeness. She pointed to Chase. "Um, do you remember Chase? He's helping Wes practice."

Brett didn't even blink at his faux pas. "Oh, yeah. Hey, Chase. Been a while since high school."

He held out a hand to Chase, who shook it, smiling. "How are you doing, Brett?"

Brett didn't even respond to the pleasantry. "Bummer about the series, huh? Too bad there's no baseball in-surance, am I right?" Brett mimed batting, and when Chase's gaze dropped, Jessica got a sick feeling in the pit of her stomach. What was Brett *doing*?

Chase said, "Yeah. Yeah, it's too bad."

She knew Chase was holding his tongue because of

her—and because Wes was just one room over, rummaging in the kitchen fridge so loudly that they could hear the jars he was clinking around all the way out in the dining room.

"Well, it's good to see you, Brett," Chase offered. To Jessica, he flashed another warm look. "I'll see you around."

"Thank you," she said, hoping the sincerity in her voice would make up for Brett's chest-beating behavior.

Chase managed a smile as he left. Jess turned from Brett, slipping away toward the kitchen without a word. She heard Brett pull up a seat at the counter, and she knew from the sound of clicking that he was making a phone call.

"Hey," she heard Brett say behind her as she pushed through the kitchen door. "Pete, it's Brett. You'll never guess who I just sold a term-life policy to!"

Chapter 9

$\mathcal{T}$HE WARM CHAMOMILE WAS JUST what Jessica needed to relax after such a long day. She scrutinized Brett over the rim of her cup. He was shoving his cell phone back into his pocket after checking his email for the fourth time since they'd gotten to her house.

Brett slung an arm over the back of the couch, his fingers brushing her shoulder. "Dinner was amazing," he said. "What was it again?"

Jessica lowered her mug. "Gnocchi with mushroom sauce."

"Mmm. Delicious." His hand was still in his pocket, and she thought she heard a faint buzz. He must have turned his alerts to vibrate. His fingers drummed on the couch cushion next to him. She could tell he wanted to get back to his phone.

Before he could, she jumped in with the idea she'd wanted to bounce off him all day. "Delicious enough to add to the diner's menu?"

Brett chuckled slightly as if she were joking. "What's wrong with the menu you have? People come to the diner for burgers and fries."

Jessica raised her mug to her lips again, waggling her eyebrows at him. "I'm thinking of mixing it up a bit." She waited for his response, ready to run and get her notebook full of ideas. Maybe Brett could help her figure out a good profit margin for her new menu items, based on the vendor pricing for the ingredients that she'd calculated so far. It seemed like a task that was right up his alley.

Brett brushed her off, changing the subject. "How about we mix it up with some of this great-looking apple pie?"

Jess glanced at the coffee table, where she'd placed one of her pies from the diner and two dessert plates. She shifted to face Brett, determined.

"No. Look, Brett, I'm serious. I've been thinking." She gathered her thoughts, searching for a way to explain all of the plans she'd been concocting since she'd seen the article in the magazine and then the food truck at the car lot. The article and the truck had reminded her of her long-waylaid idea to put the diner on wheels, and she hadn't been able to stop mulling over the possibilities. "Since Charlie keeps stealing business away, with a food truck, maybe we could just steal some of that business back."

Brett stared at her with something akin to annoyance in his eyes. He was smiling—he was *always* smiling—but she could tell that he didn't relish her bringing up an idea he'd shot down before.

"The truck idea again?" he said, his voice deceptively light.

Jessica nodded emphatically. "Yes! People love the diner; they've just forgotten about it. And with a food truck, we could remind them that we're still here. We could do ball games, and fairgrounds, and church picnics.

I could revamp our menu and have a grand reopening."

"Jess," Brett started, but she cut him off before he could launch into statistics. He would anyway, but she was set on saying what she needed to say before the numbers came raining down on her head, the weight of them squashing the dream flat.

"All I need is for you to just help me make those numbers work." There. She'd said it. He either supported her, or he'd rehash what he'd argued before—that it was impossible, that her dream required she take too big a risk.

"That's the problem, Jess. A truck's a fun idea." He patted her shoulder in what she was sure he saw as a comforting gesture—but she recognized this speech, and she found that his touch didn't comfort her. It made her angry. She'd heard everything he was about to say.

He went on, confirming her suspicions. "But it's too risky. Here." He slid the apple pie in front of them and cut a piece. "Of all new business ventures, forty percent fail right out of the gate."

He cut another piece of the pie. "And of those that survive the first year, half fail the next."

He sliced the remainder of the pie into more pieces. Jess let her mug sink to her lap. So much for the soothing comfort of chamomile. She could probably recite his wrap-up verbatim, but she let him say it anyway.

"And even if you make it that far, you have amortization on the truck, added upkeep, and costs. There's just the tiniest chance of it being truly profitable." He held up an index finger and thumb, bringing them close together, probably in case she hadn't picked up on the significance of his point from the apple pie massacre.

He stared at her, waiting for her response. Jessica just stared back.

Brett, unfazed, continued. "It's just—it's better to be safe than sorry, right? Now, how about some of this pie?"

Jessica, feeling a little crushed, said, "I'm not so hungry anymore."

"Was it something I said?" he asked absently, scooping pie onto his plate and taking a bite. Brett's pocket buzzed again. He didn't wait for her answer. He pulled out his phone and swiped to open the home screen, tapping on his email app.

I'm going to need a lot more tea, Jess thought.

The Saturday morning sunshine felt great as Chase shrugged into his jacket, jogging down the front steps to meet his dad at the lumber pile that had been delivered yesterday. Mason Taynor was already at work, squaring loose boards against the section of fence that he'd already repaired.

"Hey, there he is," his dad greeted him as Chase bent to pick up a tool belt.

Mason asked, "You're sure you're up for helping me out with this?"

Chase said, "Yeah, of course. Why would you ask?"

Mason said with a smile, "What was that you used to say all the time back in high school when I asked you to help me out? You didn't want to risk hurting your million-dollar hands."

Chase was embarrassed. He had to admit his dad was right. But Chase was determined to prove differently. "Yeah. I said a lot of dumb things back then."

The gruff, elder Taynor seemed to hesitate for a

moment, leaning on a piece of lumber as he looked at his son. "Anyway, your mother is thrilled to have you back home for once. She misses you something fierce." Chase saw something wistful in his father's expression.

Chase avoided looking at Mason, feeling a sharp sense of guilt at every ignored phone call, every unreturned email. He hadn't exactly made his parents a priority in his life lately. "I've been busy, Dad. But at least we get to see each other once every season." *Weak.* Chase knew that the lavish trips didn't make up for the birthdays, the Christmases, or the anniversaries.

Mason, his voice gentle, said, "It's great when you fly us in and put us up at those fancy hotels. That's really generous."

Uh-oh. Here comes a heart-to-heart. Chase wasn't sure he could face the way he'd treated his family since he'd gone major league, or admit that his relationship with his dad had never been the same since, either. His dad was not what one would call the sentimental type, but Chase suspected that his mother wasn't the only one who thought Chase had been away from home for far too long. It seemed that his dad thought so, too. Chase was even starting to think so.

Chase fidgeted, pushing back his jacket sleeves so they wouldn't get dirty. His gaze fell on his watch. He did a double take.

His dad continued. "We would just rather have a bit more of your time, that's all."

Wes's game. Chase's face must have reflected his panic. His dad asked, "What's the matter? You got a problem?"

Chase scrubbed a hand down his face and checked his pocket for his car keys. "Hey, don't do anything without me, all right? I'll be back in a couple hours."

Lindy came outside as Chase was sprinting toward his

convertible. Chase waved a greeting. His father sighed just before Chase hopped into the Mercedes, and Chase caught his explanation to Lindy.

"Just like old times," Mason said to her.

The truth *did* kind of hurt. Chase would have to make it up to them. He threw the car into reverse and screeched off, leaving his parents sipping coffee in the driveway. As he laid on the gas, he hoped that Officer Jake wasn't anywhere around.

The baseball game was already in progress, and Jess was squished in the stands next to Nina. They'd barely managed to save a seat for Chase, but the players were on the field and that seat, luckily, had remained empty. Jessica had asked Brett if he wanted to come to the game, hoping that they could spend some time together that didn't involve insurance or the diner, but he'd turned her down, rattling off some statistics about the probability of personal injury when one was a spectator at a sporting event. Jess didn't bother to ask Brett if he'd adjusted his odds to reflect the fact that it was youth sports.

As the minutes ticked by and Chase was still a no-show, Jess tried to keep her emotions in check. She could feel a simmering annoyance start to bubble a lot closer to anger than she liked. Wesley, who Jess noticed was almost being swallowed by his too-big uniform, walked over to the chain link fence and eyed the empty seat. His sad little face nearly broke Jess's heart.

Wesley said, "Chase isn't here? He's gonna miss my turn at bat!"

"You know what, sweetie? It's okay. You just get out there, and you do the very best you can do. Okay? You're going to be great."

Wesley smiled wanly and headed to the plate.

"All right, Wes! Come on, buddy!" Jess cheered. "You can do it!" She looked around anxiously.

Nina said, "So Chase was supposed to be here, huh?"

Jess tried to keep her voice steady. It was one thing to skip out on her, but to do it to Wes—*that* was a sure way to make her furious. "He said he would. But—"

"Hey, is this seat taken?"

Jessica looked up. Relief flooded her.

Nina hopped into the space beside her, the seat that they had been saving for Chase. That left the spot next to Jess open. Nina said slyly, "Got your name on it. Sit. Now."

Chase sat, giving Wesley, who was just getting set at home plate, a big thumbs-up. Wes's face split into a huge grin, and he returned Chase's gesture with gusto. Jess's annoyance dissolved.

Chase leaned over and whispered to Jess. She caught a subtle hint of his cologne when she scooted in to hear him, and the wash of his breath near her ear made her very aware of how close they were sitting.

"Sorry I'm late," he said, "I was fixing a fence. Don't get much of that in a downtown Boston high-rise."

"You're just in time," she replied, hoping her voice didn't sound as breathy to him as it sounded to her.

Nina leaned over and stared pointedly at Jessica. Chase luckily missed the look as he concentrated on Wes, talking to himself. "Okay, come on, buddy. Keep your eyes on the ball. Stay focused."

Jessica wrung her hands. Now was not the time for coaching. "Chase, stop talking. You're making me nervous."

Nina shushed them. "Both of you, quiet!"

On the field, Wesley steadied himself at bat. Jess watched as the pitch was thrown. She, Chase, and Nina all leaned forward in unison as Wes took a hefty swing, and with a solid *smack*, got a base hit.

"Yeah!" Chase cheered, jumping up and clapping like mad. Jess and Nina followed, springing from their seats and joining in the celebration that rose around them. Jess's heart was soaring as she watched Wes plant himself on first base.

"You taught him that?" Jess asked Chase. She studied him. He was energized. He looked happy—very different now from when she'd first seen him slumped in his car at this very field.

Chase, nudging her playfully with his shoulder, replied, "I'm just a good talent scout. The kid's a natural!"

Jessica turned her eyes back to the game, pride making her chest swell. "Way to go, Wes!" she yelled at the top of her lungs.

Chase grinned with satisfaction. He hooted and hollered into the slight breeze blowing through the stands. Jess joined in. Nina shot another significant glance her way, but Jess ignored it. Right now, Jess was happy, too—too happy to analyze a thing.

Celebrating the team's win at the diner had been Chase's idea—as had buying the whole team's burgers. Jess was glad for the business, but she'd only reluctantly accepted his offer to pay after he'd agreed to her one condition: that he come with them and let her cook him that omelet that she still owed him, on the house. Wesley's team was happily recounting their victory, play-by-play, over burgers served by a congratulatory Nina, all under the watchful eyes of their elderly coach. The man had worked with the kids' team for as long as Jess could remember. What would happen to the team when he retired next season?

Jessica and Chase sat on the window seat by the diner's broad bay window. He was close, angled toward her. As she watched the kids, Jess didn't miss where Chase's focus was. Since they'd arrived at the diner, she'd felt like she was the only person he'd looked at. He'd watched her when she'd slid behind the counter to make shakes for the team, watched her as she'd helped Nina with the first few rounds of plates that had come out of the bustling kitchen, and he watched her now as she spoke. There was an affection in his eyes that was a true blast from the past.

Jess tried not to get too caught up in the attention, but it was difficult. She checked to see if Brett had returned her text from earlier when she'd written to tell him about the team's win. There was no reply, but her phone showed that Brett had read the text just minutes after she'd sent it. She wondered dryly what the probability was that Brett had started to see Jess as a given—or maybe he was losing interest. Maybe she should ask, since statistics was Brett's area of expertise.

Jess scanned the diner and spied Wes, chatting with a table full of other players. "Well, look at that. It is so nice to see Wes bonding with his team. Finally."

Chase followed her line of sight. "It looks like the coach has everything under control." He paused. "Might go even better without his mom hovering over him for a bit?"

Jessica stammered, "But what—" Chase slid a slow, pointed look her way. She thought about it. "Fine. Maybe you're right."

Chase stood and held his hand out to Jess. She caught Nina's attention and indicated with a tilt of her head that she and Chase were going to step outside. Nina, to her credit, managed to keep a straight face as she waved Jess toward the door. Jess stood and took Chase's offered hand. He helped her up off the window seat, and she missed the warmth of his grasp when he let go.

It started raining the moment they stepped out of the diner. Dodging the drops and bantering as they ran, they made for the closest shelter—the gazebo in the nearby town square. Once under cover, Jess shook the rain from her coat. Despite the sudden shower, she was glad she had agreed to take a walk with Chase. Out here, they could at least talk without the cacophony caused by the few dozen people crammed into the diner.

Jessica said, "You know, you really hung in there with Wes. I gotta say, I'm surprised."

"Oh yeah? He's a terrific kid, and he's got real talent."

"Thank you," Jess replied. "You helped show him how to use it."

"I'm just happy I had the time." Chase turned away, studying his fingernails. Jess found the change in his focus a telling sign. She just wasn't sure what it was telling. She saw him swallow. His voice lowered as he continued. "In fact, I might even have more time to help him."

Jessica got the same sinking feeling that she'd gotten when Brett had number-punched her food truck dream into mush. "What do you mean?"

Chase took a breath that expanded his chest and then let it out slowly. "There haven't been any real offers yet. I don't know if there will be." Something in his face reminded her so strongly of Wesley—no, of Chase when he'd been younger. She remembered Chase's excitement when recruiters had started showing up at his games, remembered how uncertain he'd been, back before the fame and fortune. She saw that guy again, the one who hadn't known if he was good enough.

Jessica tried her best to reassure him. "C'mon. You're a star pitcher."

Chase attempted a smile. "Or maybe just a has-been with a fading arm."

"Your agent is still working on it, right?"

He nodded.

"Okay! Well, there's still hope." She ignored the fact that she was cheerleading for him to get pulled away from Parker Falls—from her—again.

"You always did look on the bright side," Chase remarked. But he'd started to smile again, if only a little.

Jessica laughed, but it was as halfhearted as his smile was. "I try."

The rain came down steadily, cocooning the gazebo in gray, sheeting streams, cooling the air. Jess pulled her coat a little tighter around her.

"As long as we're being honest," she said, meeting his gaze as he looked up to catch her eyes, "I'm doing all I can to be mom and dad to an eight-year-old and keep Grandpa's diner afloat while the wolves are just circling. If something doesn't change soon, I'm gonna lose the diner."

She sighed. "I've been thinking of getting a food truck to spread the word around town, and maybe even do a grand reopening for the diner, but it all just seems so risky."

She braced for Chase to make fun of her food truck idea. He was a big shot, professional athlete with a fancy car. Her small-town money troubles were probably laughable to him.

"You know what they say," he replied, shrugging. "If the batting order isn't working, you may want to switch it up."

Hearing her own words echoed back at her was a strange but welcome coincidence.

"Funny, seeing you after all these years reminds me how little my life has changed," Jessica murmured. She had to swallow down a lump in her throat.

Chase frowned. "Are you kidding me? You raised a great kid! And for me, these past fifteen years have felt almost like a dream. You look around, all these people are in your corner, and then the next minute, you wake up, and they're all gone."

The back of Jess's throat burned, and she swallowed again, this time with a bit of difficulty. She wanted to tell him how she'd felt when he'd left, but she was worried that if she did, she would start spilling out her life's story as it had unfolded since his departure—how she'd thrown herself into a relationship to forget him, how she'd had misgivings from the start and eventual regrets about Davis, about her heartache when her husband had split. She was saved from her confessions by Chase, who pointed through the rain, which was now letting up.

"Remember that lamppost?" Chase asked. "That's where we had our first kiss."

Jessica shook her head. "No, that lamppost is where

we had our first argument," she declared. She pointed at the center of the gazebo. "This is where we had our first kiss."

"Well, it's been more than fifteen years. Why don't we bury the hatchet?" Chase suggested.

Jess bristled a little at what she thought his implication was: that she was carrying a grudge. Was she? No. She'd been hurt when he'd left, but she'd moved on—at least, she thought she had. And even if she'd made a bad choice with Davis, Chase still bore some of the responsibility for their difficult parting. Maybe it was a good time to keep up with the honesty.

Jessica echoed his suggestion, adding her own two cents. "Bury the hatchet? Well, I can think of two words that would be especially helpful."

"'I'm right'?" Chase guessed.

"I was thinking more along the lines of 'I'm sorry,'" she informed him, a bit icily.

He shook his head, disbelief evident on his face. "You dropped me, Jessica, remember?"

"Only 'cause you were leaving town! And my folks needed help running the place when Grandpa got sick. And, what, were you really wanting to have me tag along on the road?"

Chase raked a hand through his hair. "Yes!" As if the emphatic word had slipped out without his permission, Chase cleared his throat. "Why not? You were always a dreamer. Wasn't your yearbook quote about traveling the globe?"

Jessica shot back, "Well, life didn't quite end up that way. And, anyhow, Davis ended up being dreamer enough for us both. Someone had to stay and pay the bills. So here I am, like one of those pies in the display case at the diner, adventurous, but just going around and around."

They both stared at each other. She found herself, embarrassingly, fighting back the burn in her throat again. This time, she hadn't caught it before it had reached her eyes. "Chase, once you left, you never even contacted me. Not once. That was the part that really hurt."

He seemed to accept what she'd said, and his eyes entreated her forgiveness. "I know it's years too late, but I'm sorry," he said.

Jess could hear the sincerity in his voice. "Me, too."

Jessica knew that she had been just as much at fault in their breakup as Chase. She could have picked up the phone in the last fifteen years—heck, she saw his parents on a regular basis around town—but she never had. She'd been proud. She hadn't wanted Chase to know she'd never lived the glamorous life he seemed to lead, never had the fairy tale she'd been so sure she was running to with Davis. And she could never tell Chase that she had the scariest feeling that seeing him again was starting to change her—change what she was willing to risk.

Chase offered a hand. "Peace?"

Jessica reached out and shook it. "Done. And thank you."

The rain had stopped. Just like at the diner, Chase's hand lingered, wrapped around hers. He rubbed his thumb over the back of her hand. Her breath caught. Her phone rang. She pulled away, perhaps a bit too abruptly.

Peeking at her phone, she felt immediately guilty. "It's Brett. I'd better take this."

Chase nodded, standing. "And I'd better check in with my, uh, Heather. See you at practice tomorrow."

She looked up from her phone, surprised. "You've helped so much already. I couldn't take up more of your time."

"I promised Wes. And the week's not over yet." Chase ambled down the gazebo steps as she answered her call. She brought the phone to her ear.

"Brett? Hi!" she said.

"Babe," Brett groaned, and Jess could tell by the sounds in the background that he was still at the office. On a Saturday night.

"I know that I was only planning on popping into the office for a bit today," he started.

Jessica sighed. Chase smiled back over his shoulder at her and gave her a wave as he headed toward the diner.

Chapter 10

$\mathscr{I}$T WAS DARK BY THE time Chase made it back to his parents' house. His headlights illuminated the perfectly constructed new fence that now stood beside the house, and then swept brightly over the figure of his father, who was just picking up the last of his tools. Chase realized with a start that it was well past the time he'd promised to return, and he hadn't even called to explain to his folks why he'd bolted so suddenly.

Chase shut off the car and climbed out, calling to Mason. "Dad, what are you doing? I was going to help you."

"I think I'm done." Chase was surprised that his dad didn't seem angry. In fact, his father's voice had the same gentleness to it that had been there earlier, when he'd started to talk to Chase about being home.

Chase racked his brain for a way to help. "Well, let me take care of the painting, at least," he implored.

Mason smiled at his son. "Don't worry about it. You always had bigger things on your mind." Mason clapped Chase on the shoulder and hefted the toolbox. Though he knew his dad was ribbing him, Chase couldn't help but feel his guilt multiply as Mason suggested, "Why don't you go wash up those million-dollar hands for dinner?"

Chase watched his dad walk off. Chase had forgotten about his mom cooking dinner. The omelet from the diner rolled in his stomach as he headed into the house.

Jessica tucked Wes in, settling next to him on the narrow twin bed and petting his hair, awed at how remarkable her little guy was turning out to be. Wes gazed sleepily up at Jess.

"You ready for bed, sweetie?" she asked.

Wesley nodded, but something was on his mind. Jess looked questioningly at him.

He said, "You smile at Chase. A lot."

Jessica laughed. "Well, maybe that's because he makes you smile, and that makes me happy. And I'm proud of you. You were really great today."

"I had a great coach." Wesley said, yawning.

Jessica agreed. "You're right. He is great."

"I wasn't talking about Chase," Wes replied.

It was comments like this that made everything Jess did worthwhile. She was so impressed with Wes, with his hard work despite their setbacks, with what he had accomplished.

"All right, mister. Time for bed." She switched off the light and kissed Wesley on the forehead.

Wesley's voice was heavy, sleepy. "I love you."

Jessica said, "I love you more."

Despite her own exhaustion, as she snuck out of his room, she couldn't fight a smile.

After his flub on the repair project yesterday, Chase was determined to paint the fence today. He pushed open the heavy glass door of the town's hardware store, on a mission to find the particular brands of paint and primer that his dad liked.

Chase approached the counter and caught the attention of the clerk, Bob, who'd worked there for as long as Chase could remember.

"Hi, how you doing? Do you know where I can find the primer? Got to paint the fence."

Bob beamed at Chase. "For Chase Taynor, I'll walk ya there myself. Come on."

"Thanks, man," Chase said, grinning back. He remembered that Bob had always been a huge baseball fan, and he was grateful that Bob hadn't asked about the series or Chase's plans for next season.

Chase followed Bob, who hustled toward a display.

Chase heard a voice behind him. "Hey, Chase."

Chase turned to see Brett. "Hey, Brett."

Ugh. As much as Chase had paid lip service to Brett being a nice guy, his opinion of the man had been formed fifteen years ago—and judging by their run-in at the diner, some of the nice seemed to have worn off. Chase wondered what Brett was doing at the hardware store in the middle of a Sunday, dressed in a suit.

"How ya doing?" Brett asked.

Chase did not relish the idea of having a prolonged conversation with Brett, especially since he'd found his thoughts turning more and more to Jess today—most of them having nothing to do with Wes or baseball.

"Pretty good," Chase managed. "Yourself?" *Dang it.* His polite upbringing had just extended the conversation.

Brett seemed as though he'd been waiting for Chase to ask, responding a little too enthusiastically. "I'm great! Great! Business is booming. Baseball seasons, they may come and go, but people always need insurance."

Chase bit back on a likely unwise reply and said, "Uh, yeah, that's true." He craned to look around Brett, hoping that Jess was with him and might rescue him from whatever agenda Brett had for engaging Chase in conversation. Chase wasn't that lucky.

"Listen," Brett said, adopting an extra-patronizing tone when he next spoke, rankling Chase even further, "I really appreciate you helping Wesley."

Chase nodded. Maybe it was just *him*. Maybe he was inclined not to like the guy because he was starting to feel something for Jess. Maybe Brett was being sincere. But as far as Chase knew, Brett hadn't ever coached Wes. Chase hadn't seen the man at any of Wes's recent practices, and he hadn't come to Wes's big game. It was odd that Brett would take an interest in Chase being involved if his concern was for the kid.

"We're having a great time," Chase said. "He's a terrific kid."

Brett quickly changed the subject, getting to what Chase knew was Brett's real concern. "So, when are you headed out of town? That arm still got some miles left in it?" Brett pantomimed a pitch. It was just as grating as when he'd mock batted back at the diner.

Chase said evenly, "The jury's still out."

"Well, fingers crossed you'll be on your way soon." Brett smiled, and Chase got the message.

"Yeah," Chase replied, holding out a hand to Brett. "Good to see you."

Brett glanced down at Chase's offered hand and ignored it. He flashed one last, cold smile at Chase before he turned and sauntered toward the exit. Chase shook his head, looking over to see Bob standing by the primers, staring. *Great.* It was a small town. Who knew what gossip would fly from *that* exchange?

"All right," Chase said to Bob, walking over and surveying the shelves. "So what do we got here?"

After priming and painting the fence, Chase hurried to the ball field. At this practice, Chase was playing catcher, opting for the first half of their time together to have Wesley on the mound.

They weren't accomplishing much, and Chase couldn't ignore where Wes's attention was directed. The boy constantly scanned over to watch the other kids in the park, practicing with their fathers. Wesley's subsequent pitches went wide, wild, or just bounced ineffectually toward home plate.

Wes wound up and fired again, this time sending the baseball soaring over Chase's head.

Chase, a little exasperated, said, "Hello?"

Wesley appeared far away, off in another world.

Chase said, "Wes, baseball takes focus. What's on your mind?"

Wesley didn't say anything for a moment. "Dad and me used to practice here almost every day after school. Did your dad teach you baseball?"

Chase started walking over to Wes, almost automatically. If Wes was going to confide in Chase, he wanted to make sure that no one overheard what they were talking about. Chase smiled slightly as he walked. He was starting to kind of understand the fierce, protective urge that Jess felt in spades for the little guy in front of him.

Chase stopped when he was close enough that no one would likely hear. "Yeah," he told Wes. "In fact, he taught me how to throw my first curveball. Then, in junior high, my coach took over, and my dad kind of stepped back."

Was that when Chase had started to forget how much his dad had done for him? He pushed aside the troubling thought.

Chase tossed Wesley the ball. "It's good to have those memories."

Wes still didn't look convinced. Chase remembered how he'd felt about playing ball when he had first started out. He tried another angle, knowing that Wesley hadn't known much that he could count on, aside from Jessica, in the past few years.

"Anyway, the way I see it, even when things change and life gets tricky, baseball's still there for you," Chase told him.

Wesley studied Chase for a moment. Was that a crack forming in the boy's skeptical expression? "How do you know that?" Wesley asked.

"Oh, personal experience." *Very personal.* With a pleasant jolt of realization, Chase recognized that he'd spoken the truth. The game *was* still there, pure and exciting, despite his own career troubles.

Wesley said, "So nobody wants to pick you for their team, huh?" Wes was now feeling sorry for Chase. At least it was better than the kid feeling sorry for himself.

"Yeah, that pretty much nails it," Chase admitted, amused.

"Maybe you gotta be patient, too," Wes said sagely.

Chase smirked. "So now you're giving *me* the advice?"

Wesley said impishly, "Somebody has to. Mom says you never listen."

Chase threw back his head and laughed. "Oh she does, does she?"

"Yeah." Wes dissolved into a fit of giggles.

"Oh yeah?" Chase made a mental note to give Jess a *really* hard time about that little comment when he saw her later.

He realized that in the next week, there would come a time when there would be no "later" with her. The thought shook him up in a way that he couldn't quite explain.

Wesley grew quiet. As if he could read Chase's mind, he said, "She also says you're leaving soon. Is that true?"

A little sadly, Chase replied, "Yeah, it's true." He tried to lighten the mood, socking Wes softly on the shoulder with his mitt. "But until then, I say we have as much fun as possible."

Wesley got into position and put on his game face. Chase crouched and waited for Wes's pitch. Wes wound up and let the ball fly. A second later, the ball smacked solidly into the middle of Chase's glove.

Chapter 11

$\mathcal{J}$ESSICA LEFT HER ROOM AFTER getting ready for her birthday date. She took care to select a sleek pencil skirt that she knew Brett liked. She was carefully navigating down the stairs in her high heels, just putting on a shimmering pair of earrings, when her phone rang. She hurried to scoop it off the kitchen table and smiled as she answered.

"Hey, Brett!" She was excited to be trying out the restaurant he'd chosen. She knew the diner was no five-star destination, but she might be able to pick up a few touches to add to her notebook of ideas.

"Hi, Jess. How you doing?" She brushed off the feeling that his voice sounded odd. Maybe he'd had a long day. Maybe a little flirting would cheer him up.

Jessica replied sassily, "Great. And looking especially good tonight, if I do say so myself."

"Look, I'm so sorry, hon." Brett plowed past her banter without acknowledging it. "But the owner of Bacon Barrel called me and wants to meet up to talk coverage for all eighteen of his locations. Can we take a rain check on tonight?"

Jessica tried extra hard to keep the disappointment out of her voice. It was her birthday, for goodness' sake! She felt the distance between her and Brett stretch a little bit wider.

"Sure, that's okay," she said. "My grandpa always said, 'When opportunity knocks, better answer.'"

"Thanks, Jess," Brett replied with a note of relief. "We'll celebrate even bigger next weekend, okay? And meantime, I had a present sent over. You might want to peek out your front door. Just a little something I found."

Jessica felt her mood buoy a bit. What a sweet gesture. Would it be a huge bouquet of roses? Takeout from the restaurant that they were going to miss dining at? A food truck parked in her driveway?

She looked out front and saw a big box on her doorstep. Festooned with pink ribbons, the box still bore the price sticker from the hardware store.

"Wow, an air purifier." She tried her best to seem excited. It was the thought that counted...right? "I don't know quite what to say."

Brett said, "I have the exact same one. It really helps with my allergies. And you said that yours make you snore. Happy birthday!" She could hear the glee in his voice. She could almost see him checking off "successful birthday gift for Jess" on a to-do list somewhere.

"Thank you," she said. At least her manners were still functioning, even if she was stammering for a response.

With a promise to call her the second he knew whether he'd landed the Bacon Barrel account, Brett hung up. Jess set her cell phone down on her entry table. With a resigned sigh, she teetered a bit on her fancy heels as she bent to drag the bulky cardboard box into her house.

Jess was overdressed for the couch, but she didn't care. It wasn't often that she got to wear an outfit that made her feel the way this one did, so she'd chosen to keep it on rather than hang it back up and climb into her too-big, self-pity pajamas. Picking up the last of the yearbooks she'd unearthed from her closet, she was surprised when a small stack of postcards slipped from somewhere between the pages and fluttered to the carpet. She scooped them up, laying the yearbook over her lap. The postcards were all faded photos of far-off places: Rome, Paris, Tunisia. She'd collected the blank cards—from the post office in town—since her early teens.

She flipped through the postcards, feeling a pang of wistfulness before she tucked them back in. Thumbing through the pages of the yearbook, Jess came to a layout featuring a photo of her and Chase as Spring Fling King and Queen. If things hadn't ended with Chase precisely the way they had, she wouldn't have Wes, so there was no earthly way she would ever change a single decision she'd made back then. But now? Chase was here now, and she still felt the same spark that she'd felt all those years ago.

She stared at the picture of the two of them, remembering the hurt in his voice at the gazebo.

You dropped me, Jessica, remember?

Did it still affect him, even after all these years? She scanned the picture once more. Her as a brunette and Chase with his goofy spiked hair. Their color-coordinated outfits. She laughed, allowing the memories for just another moment before she snapped out of it.

"Wake up, Jessica. In a week, he'll be gone." And she would be hurt if she got too attached. She couldn't risk that, not again.

The front door opened, and Chase and Wesley came in, laughing. Jess shut the yearbook quickly, shifting it off to one side of the couch before the two of them could make it to the doorway of the living room.

As they came into view from the foyer, Chase spotted Jess.

"Hey," he said, all smiles.

"Hey," she replied, recognizing the feeling that bloomed at the sight of him but pushing it back.

Wesley looked confused. "Mom? I thought I had the babysitter."

"Something came up for Brett, so we postponed." It was a little disconcerting how often she had to keep her voice from giving away how she felt lately.

Chase's lips drew into a tight line. "Sorry to hear that."

"That's okay," she assured him.

"Happy birthday," Chase said with a playful smile. He'd always hated it when she was down. Ever since they'd been kids, he'd been able to make her laugh, no matter her mood.

"Thank you." She seriously hoped he wasn't about to burst into song. He'd done that to her once, in the middle of the diner when they'd been dating, and it had been mortifying—*and*, admittedly, pretty cute. They stared at each other for a beat too long before Chase broke away, looking rattled.

"All right, guys. Well, good night," he said, lifting a hand.

Wes grabbed for Chase's jacket. "Wait. Mom, what're we doing for dinner?"

Jessica shrugged. "We just have leftovers in the fridge.

I thought I'd heat them up."

Wesley motioned to Chase, who bent his ear to her son. It was the same move that Wes had used to needle Jess into asking Chase to coach him. What was that little schemer up to? She couldn't hear what Wes was saying as he whispered something to Chase.

"Well, I'm game," Chase responded to Wesley, "but we're going to have to ask your mom."

Jessica was highly suspicious of their plotting and unsure if she was going to like the question. "Ask me what?"

Chase said, "Well, since it is your birthday…"

Wesley added, "And you're always cooking for everyone else at the diner…"

Chase finished. "When was the last time somebody made you dinner?"

Chase and Wesley smiled big Cheshire grins in unison. Jess eyed the two of them lounging in the doorway. She felt her good mood returning, and the same warmth filled her chest for both of them. When her eyes settled on Chase's again, she knew that she was in some serious trouble.

Chase couldn't remember the last time he'd felt as relaxed as he was now. Sitting at Jessica's kitchen table, surrounded by her and Wes's laughter, he felt inexplicably at home.

Finishing the last bite of her second helping, Jess said, "So Mr. Million Dollar Arm can cook now. And vegetarian lasagna, no less."

Chase shot back teasingly, "There're lots of new sides

to me you don't know about yet."

Yet? Where had that come from? Was he planning on showing them to her?

"Is that so?" Jess's sparkling eyes were brighter than the earrings that winked from her earlobes. Chase had been distracted by her the second he'd seen her on the couch. She had left her date night outfit on, and despite the fact that it should have reminded Chase that she was off-limits, he couldn't help but be captivated by how beautiful she was.

Chase, leaning back in his chair, said, "Sure, like how I learned to cook on the road. When the team bus pulls in late and room service is closed, you have to get creative—and fast. I'll have you know I once transformed minibar peanuts, coffee creamer, and instant noodles to make an epic pad thai."

At that, both Jess and Wesley gave in to another round of giggling.

Jessica said, "I have to admit, I'm impressed. Your supermodel must think you're quite the catch."

Chase was taken aback as realization struck at Jess's statement. "Actually, I've never even cooked for her. I don't even know if she eats." He knew one thing, though. Heather still hadn't returned any of his calls.

It was getting late. Chase knew he should be getting up, helping to clear the plates, getting out of their hair. But Jess made no move to stand, gave no indication that he wasn't welcome to stay as long as he wanted to. Was this what it was like being in their everyday? The way he was feeling tonight, he had to admit that he might not mind a life like this. The thought was a little scary... and a little exhilarating.

Wesley's voice broke into Chase's thoughts. "That was fun today, coach. We're on again for tomorrow, right?"

"You bet, champ."

Wesley hesitated, looking as though he wanted to ask Chase something. Jess, who had been studying Chase a little more closely than he'd noticed before, turned to her son.

"What's going on?" she asked Wes.

"Something else, Wesley?" Chase prompted.

Wesley said, "Well, kind of. I mean..." Again, the boy hesitated.

Chase tried to reassure him. "You can say it, pal. What's on your mind?"

Wesley rushed on as if he might lose the courage to speak unless he pushed forward. "Will you play in my father-son baseball game on Friday?"

Jess tutted softly, starting to interject, but Wes plowed ahead. "I know you're not my dad, but the other kids'll have theirs and…" Wes trailed off, his eyes dropping.

Chase's heart felt like it was being squeezed in his chest. He saw Jess put her hand to her own heart, and Chase knew that she must have felt the poignancy of what Wes was asking even more acutely than Chase did. Chase blinked. He was moved, and he had to clear his throat a bit before answering.

Jessica spoke first. She explained softly, "Sweetie, he's probably going to be gone by then."

Chase made up his mind as Jess attempted to let Wes down easy. She was likely trying to give Chase an out, too. He didn't need—didn't *want*—an out.

"I'd love to be there. It'd be an honor."

Wesley's face lit up, and his chair scraped the tile as he threw it back and dashed over to hug Chase, catching Chase off guard. As Wes's arms came around Chase's neck and his dark head crashed into Chase's shoulder, Chase thought about his own dad. Mason had played many father-son games with Chase, had spent many hours on the ball field teaching him. Wes had an absent father, something that Chase had never had to experience. Until now, Chase hadn't realized how blessed he'd been.

"Thanks, Chase," Wes said, squeezing tight and burrowing into Chase's shoulder a bit harder. Chase hugged Wes back. He guessed his bad shoulder was still good for something, and the thought made him smile.

Chase said, "You bet, pal."

Chase's eyes flicked up to Jess. Her eyes were starting to mist.

She swiped at her cheeks and said cheerfully, "Well. I think the only thing missing is dessert."

"Wish I could whip up birthday cake," Chase said apologetically.

Wesley piped up. "I know where we can get a funnel cake."

Chase was already reaching for his keys.

The music and scents filling the evening air seemed magically identical to the ones that Jessica remembered from her time as Spring Queen. She hadn't realized it, but she'd avoided the Fling for years after Chase had left. She remembered her excuses—too busy, too corny—but as she and Chase strolled together, holding funnel cakes, and Wesley ran ahead to watch a juggling act that was starting on stage, she knew why she'd stayed away. Too many memories of Chase and how they'd both been so young and so immature.

Jessica said, "Thank you so much for spending time

with Wesley. Not having his dad around the past two years has not been easy on him."

"No thanks needed. He's great," Chase assured her. They slowed to a stop and watched the juggler as she added several more brightly colored balls into an already impressive number flying in a dizzying circle.

"So, any nibbles from the baseball world?" Jess wasn't certain if she should bring the subject up, but since Chase had offered to stay for Wes's game, her curiosity was piqued. Staying for the father-son game would definitely put Chase past the time he'd said he'd be in town. In fact, it nearly doubled the length of stay that he'd told her that first day at the diner.

"Nibbles, but that's about it. Maybe it's all for the best." Chase didn't sound as upset about the prospect of not returning to professional sports as he had the last time they'd talked about it.

"What do you mean?" Was Chase thinking of giving up the limelight? *Could* he? Jess tried to see the cocky guy from television in the man standing next to her, but all she saw was Chase—the old Chase.

Chase said, "Where's all that glory gotten me? Fifteen years gone, and my dad just thinks I'm full of myself. And maybe I was. Or am."

Jessica snorted a bit indelicately. "Come on. Deep down, your dad is proud of you. There's no way he couldn't be." She took the last bite of her funnel cake as they started walking again.

"I don't know about that. Ever since I hit pro, we just—we don't get along."

"Well," Jess suggested, "maybe you're just out of practice."

He looked sideways at her, amused. She thought her little life-coaching moment had been pretty spot-on. A moment passed, and they both laughed.

They strolled by some fairgoers handing out sparklers. Jess grabbed Chase's empty plate and deposited his and hers into a nearby trash can.

Chase dusted his hands together, shaking off errant bits of sugar. "You know, I'd forgotten how friendly everyone here is."

Jessica nodded. "I know Parker Falls isn't Boston, but there's a reason people love it." She sighed, and answering his inquisitive glance, she said, "I just wish I could figure out the diner part of the puzzle. Things are getting desperate."

"Listen, Jess, if you need money—" He didn't look a bit uncomfortable as he said it, but she was instantly aghast at the thought.

Call it pride, but she cut him off, waving away his suggestion. "No, no, no. That's such a sweet offer, but if there's a way that I can put in the work to fix this, I will."

He didn't push her, instead narrowing his eyes and lapsing into a thoughtful silence.

"Well, what about your food truck idea?" he finally asked. "I mean, you said yourself everyone loves the diner. Maybe they just need to be reminded of it. And a food truck could give you more visibility. And you could do that grand reopening."

Jessica heard Brett's voice in her head, and the image of a hacked-up apple pie invaded Chase's well-intentioned pep talk. "Yeah, I don't know. I am barely hanging on as it is."

They reached a lemonade vendor, and Chase bought two, offering one of the yellow-festooned cups to Jess. She sipped experimentally, glad that the drink was sweet since she was suddenly feeling sour.

"I mean, maybe Brett's right," she volunteered. "Doubling

down on a food truck is not a good idea."

Chase made a face when she mentioned Brett's name, but she didn't dare ask why. Chase hadn't talked too much about Heather, but Jess knew trouble was brewing there, so she certainly didn't want to spill out all her doubts about her relationship with Brett. That would be an invitation to commiserate on romantic woes, and she and Chase didn't need *more* to bond over. Wes's game would come and go, and then, very possibly, Chase would be back to the big leagues. Jess couldn't hang any hopes on him sticking around Parker Falls, no matter how much her heart seemed to be nudging her toward him.

"Oh, come on, Jess. You've got to take a chance," Chase implored.

"Chase Taynor," she teased, "always rolling the dice."

Wes scampered up to them, looking a bit disheveled and more than a little tired. Jess knew it was time to go home. Wes and Chase had treated her like a fairy tale princess tonight, but she was looking at a kid who was about to turn into a grumpy pumpkin. She handed Wes her lemonade and put her arm around his shoulder. She nudged Chase, and they all started toward the exit.

"Hey, look. I'll help you out," Chase said, "and not with a loan. You just tell me what you need me to do, and I'll be there."

Jessica was firm. "Thank you. But I have been standing on my own two feet for a very long time now."

"Believe me, I can see that," he replied. "But I got my hands free, and this will give me a chance to make up for the past."

They passed a game booth near the door where people were stepping up to hurl balls at a pyramid of metal milk bottles. The game booth operator called out to Chase, "How about you, sir?"

Chase waved at the man. "Oh, no. I'm okay."

Wesley disentangled from Jess and grabbed Chase's hand, dragging him to the booth. "Chase, you've got to!"

The small crowd that had been milling around began to gather and grow. Chase rolled his eyes, looking to Jess for help. She shrugged, as if to say, *The kid's right.*

Chase relented. "Okay, okay!" He shot a dirty look her way, but his eyes were smiling. The barker gave Chase three balls, and he handed two to Wes, who stood by, ready to assist. As sleepy as Wes had appeared a few moments ago, he was wide awake now. Jess knew that no matter what happened when Chase left Parker Falls, she would always be grateful to him for making Wesley happy, if only for this short time.

Chase wound up and hurled the first ball. It missed. The game booth operator hollered out a whooping, "Nope!"

Chase laughed. Jessica flashed an encouraging smile. Wes offered up another ball, which Chase studied for a moment and tossed up a few times. He rolled his shoulder before throwing the second ball. The barker drew out his sarcastically sympathetic reaction.

"Ahh, sorry, bud!"

Another miss. Jess was surprised that Chase didn't appear the least bit fazed. Wes looked more nervous than his coach as Chase prepared for the last pitch. Pausing dramatically, Chase's attention drifted to Jessica. She swore she could see the sparkling lights of the festival winking back at her in his eyes. She could almost see him as he'd been all those years ago, playing this same game to win her a giant stuffed tiger.

The crowd around them seemed to be holding their collective breath. Chase leaned a bit toward her and whispered, "Do you mind just moving out of my line of sight?"

Jessica fought a smile. If she smiled much more tonight, her face would crack. "Hmm? Why?"

Chase said, "You're just a bit of a distraction."

The smile won out. She took a step back. "Oh. Okay. This good?"

Chase flicked his fingers at her, indicating that she should keep backing up. She had to fight not to laugh as she tiptoed backward. The crowd behind her parted and then closed back in front of her, blocking him completely from her view.

"Perfect!" he shouted.

She couldn't see the throw, but she heard the milk cans fall musically as Chase hurled the ball and knocked down the entire pyramid. The crowd cheered—Wesley loud enough that Jess could hear him over all the others.

The game booth operator was somehow able to yell over the cacophony, "We have a winner!"

Jess pushed back through the crowd to see Chase pointing at his prize selection. Wes stood beside Chase, beaming.

Chase said, "Phew. That was more stressful than game seven." The booth operator handed Chase a huge stuffed tiger, which he held out to Jessica. Her world tilted just a little.

"For you," Chase said. "It's not much of a birthday present, but—"

"Thanks," she managed as she took it, her throat constricting. "It's perfect."

Chapter 12

*N*INA GABBED AWAY AS SHE and Jessica made their way down the kitchen supply aisle at the hardware store. Jess, lost in thought, blocked the chatter of her friend out until she heard Nina stop behind her. Jess glanced back as Nina held up an odd-looking cooking utensil.

Nina said, "What exactly is this, again?"

Jessica took the implement and tossed it back and forth in her hands. "New silicone spatula. Lightweight. Good grip. Colorful. Or…"

Jess grabbed what she had come for off a wall rack, examining it. "Or the old, standard metal flipper." Jess frowned at the utensil in her hand.

Jess felt, rather than saw, Nina look at her as if she were speaking a foreign language. "Good to have choices, right?" Nina asked.

Jessica hummed noncommittally. They continued down the aisle, but Jess didn't look at anything else. She was having the worst time deciding—and for goodness' sake, they were *spatulas*.

Nina, hauling their empty shopping basket, sauntered alongside Jess. "Speaking of which, how are things with, ya know, Brett?"

Jessica said, "It's fine."

Nina narrowed her eyes at Jess, and Jess wondered what had been wrong with her response.

"Okay," Nina said, sounding slightly annoyed, "now that we've got 'fine' out of our system, why don't you tell your old friend the truth?" Nina plucked a kitchen tool from one of the last pegs on the aisle, studying it and giving Jess time to respond.

Jessica spun and faced Nina, sighing. "Things are fine. Brett is"—she hesitated, searching for the right word—"Brett."

Nina added, "Very dependable and pretty cute in a total nerdy kind of way?" Nina thought Brett was *cute*? Yeah, he was, but Jess didn't agree that he'd been dependable lately. Unless she turned into a cubicle, she feared that she and Brett weren't destined for the long haul. Had she even ever wanted that?

"And then there's Chase," Nina breathed. Her face lit as she made the connection between spatulas and Jess's angst. "Wow. Whoa. Yeah, yeah. Whoa! This is not about spatulas at all, is it?"

Jessica let out an exasperated huff, shaking her head. How ridiculous that she was reaching some kind of crisis point over kitchen tools at the hardware store. And she was about to spill her guts to her best friend, soundtracked by the cheerful sounds of the glass insect wind chimes hanging in the window behind her. But Jess guessed that this was as good a place as any.

"I don't know, Nina. I just…I've been thinking lately that maybe the last couple of years I've just been playing it safe."

"What do you mean?" Nina asked, her face serious. Jess felt a swell of love for her quirky friend. Nina wouldn't care if Jess had a nervous breakdown and walked into the diner wearing a lampshade on her head. Nina would just duck under the shade and ask Jess what was up.

"Well, I've had two guys leave town on me: Wesley's dad and Chase. And maybe that's why I've picked the most reliable man in the world. And I've been serving the same menu my grandpa did forty years ago."

Nina prodded Jess gently. "So what are you saying?"

Jessica said, "The diner's hanging on by a thread anyway." Excited by her sudden resolve, Jess felt a slow smile begin. Nina began to smile, too. Recalling the bad advice she'd given Chase about not getting Wes's hopes up, and flashing back to Brett's depressing speech with the apple pie, Jess felt her conviction strengthen.

"Maybe it's high time I swung for the fences," Jess said.

Nina's giggling followed Jess all the way to the registers. "Do you even know how to play baseball?" Nina asked.

Jess plunked both of the spatulas onto the conveyor belt at a register and turned to face Nina. "No, I don't," she admitted. "But I do know a good coach."

Chase had been surprised when his cell phone had rung and the screen had flashed Jessica's name. He'd picked up immediately, convincing himself that the speed was just because he was afraid he'd missed something they'd scheduled. When she'd asked for his help, he'd agreed even faster than he'd answered her call. Her laughter, if possible, was even more attractive over the phone.

"You're asking me for help, and now you're *laughing* at me?" he'd teased.

"No, no," she'd said, stifling the sounds. "I just didn't expect you to be so easy."

"Well," Chase had replied, "I know it isn't easy for you to ask. But thank you for calling me. Tell me what you need."

Fifteen minutes later, he and Jessica approached the edge of the car lot, scoping out the rusty food truck. Chase felt like they were back in high school, plotting practical jokes, as they passed the truck's bumper and exchanged sneaky smiles.

Jessica said, "Okay. This is going to call for some teamwork."

"Yeah," Chase said, nodding to her. He was definitely in. No way was this salesman going to pull a fast one on them as a team.

"You do your part, and I'll handle the rest," she instructed. Chase, whose first instinct when she'd explained where they were meeting had been to try to convince Jess to let him handle the sale, had stopped himself from insisting, instead listening as she'd hatched her plan. And he had to admit she sounded like she was well prepared. Now all he had to do was be her wingman.

"Okay. Let's do this." They high-fived. Chase slid open the passenger's side door of the truck and bounded up the single step to the interior.

Her voice dropped to a whisper. "Here he comes."

Chase watched through the grimy front window as the salesman jogged toward them. The man's face lit up. Chase wasn't sure if the guy had spotted him yet.

The salesman greeted Jess with a wide, sharky grin. "Hey, hey, hey, hey! Hello again. You're back." He nodded to the truck. "I guess you couldn't forget about this baby, could you?"

Chase swung down from the truck's cab, landing by

Jess and turning to the salesman with an affable smile plastered on his face.

"Or maybe you couldn't forget about Jessica," Chase offered. "I can understand that problem." Chase winked her way, and she demurred. He addressed the salesman. "You seem like a man who really wants to make a deal."

The salesman was agape. "You're Chase Taynor!"

Chase nodded, conjuring up his best haughty expression.

The salesman stammered, "Of course, I'm always up for a deal but—"

Chase didn't wait for the man to finish. He turned his back and walked away, strolling around the perimeter of the truck. Jess tagged along silently. Chase tried to fight his amusement. She was a sneaky little thing.

Chase called over his shoulder, "Good, 'cause I can see from the way that this truck is sitting that the struts need work."

"Struts?" the salesman asked, playing dumb.

Chase nodded. He'd learned a bit more from his dad than just baseball. Being the son of a darned good mechanic had served Chase well growing up when he'd had car trouble, and now Chase found that a lot of his dad's expert tutelage on the nuts and bolts of cars had really stuck.

Jess parroted, "Hmmm. Yeah, the struts."

Chase did an about-face and brushed past the salesman, who looked a bit bulldozed. As he passed the man, Chase gave him a clap on the shoulder and a patronizing smile. Squatting near the front tire, Chase pointed under the truck. "Yeah, and there's a puddle underneath there. It looks like the coolant reservoir has got some issues, too."

"Minor adjustment," the salesman assured Jess, as if

she would be the easiest one to convince.

Jessica stepped in front of Chase. "I'll take it from here," she said. The salesman stepped in closer to Jess and put his arm around her shoulder, boxing out Chase.

"Listen, honey—" he started.

She brushed his arm off and drew the notebook from inside her coat. She gave the salesman a withering look that even made Chase stand up a little straighter as he rose from his crouch beside the truck. Chase observed amusedly as Jessica smiled at the salesman with all the sweetness she could fake.

"From what I've seen of how you tip at the diner, I think you could really use this sale," she informed him. The salesman's mouth flopped open and then snapped closed, like a fish gasping for air on dry land.

Jessica added brightly, "But I'm in sales myself, so I'm willing to deal. Based on my associate's assessment, and since I checked the Blue Book, this is my offer. Take it or leave it." She handed the salesman a sheet of paper with a price written on it.

This time, it was Chase's turn to stand silently behind her, letting Jess become the bulldozer—a true force to be reckoned with. She had definitely caught the salesman off guard. The other man gawked down at the paper. He held up a finger toward Jess, shaking his head, still trying to grasp whatever shreds of control he thought he still had in the situation.

"Well, but what you fail to consider is—" he began.

Jessica's voice was solid steel as she cut him off. "Nope. I considered it all. The question is—have you?"

Chase considered, comically, that he might be there to protect the poor man from Jess. The thought made him smirk. The salesman gulped, studied the paper again, and finally, grudgingly nodded his head.

The salesman said, "I'll go write it up."

"Thank you," Jess said, in an over-the-top, fawning tone.

"Good man," Chase said, watching as the salesman shuffled off toward the office, still looking as if he wasn't sure what had hit him. *It was the feisty blonde*, Chase wanted to remind him. And Chase was beginning to know the feeling.

As the salesman disappeared, Jessica looked over at Chase. Her eyes sparkled. Her joy was contagious. Chase was thrilled to have been even part of the reason that she was so happy.

"Now *that* was teamwork," Chase said, holding out a fist. Jess bumped it with her own and then impulsively threw her arms around him, hugging him tightly. Flashes went off in Chase's brain as bright as the lights over the field in Fenway Park. It took a beat, but he returned her tight embrace, wrapping her up against him. Her hair was soft against his cheek. He took in a breath, one that carried with it the scent of her shampoo. Jess's hands slid down his sides to rest at his waist.

A long moment passed. They only broke apart when the salesman returned, clearing his throat. Chase stepped back, and Jess reached up to smooth her hair where he'd pressed against it.

"I'm ready whenever you are," the salesman said. Jess squared her shoulders and followed the man back to the sales office. Chase hung back, knowing she'd probably appreciate privacy while getting the paperwork together. Besides, he needed a little time to catch his own, suddenly difficult, breath.

Jessica was elated—even if she was having a nerve-wracking time piloting at the wheel of the rusty, chugging food truck. At least she had Chase riding shotgun. One of the mirrors was missing from the truck's passenger side, so if she needed to switch lanes, he leaned out to make sure the way was clear. Currently, though, they were on a straightaway, so he was busy swiping furiously on his phone.

"Well," he said, "we've got our work cut out for us. But I found a guy who is two towns over who'll overhaul the engine in exchange for some autographed baseballs."

Jess shook her head and cut a look his way that he missed, being so engrossed in the texts that were flying back and forth. She'd refused a loan from him, so he was finding ways to "pay" for things that didn't involve any real money. Sneaky, but at least it was some sort of middle ground that she could live with.

Jess was glad that Chase's attention was occupied. She wished hers was—at least with something other than sitting next to him, too aware of the fact that the truck contained just the two of them. The hug at the dealership had been something she'd launched into without a thought, but now she couldn't *stop* thinking about it.

Jess said a little prayer that when they arrived at their destination—one she hadn't quite revealed to Chase—the element of surprise would be on her side and he wouldn't get mad. She made a turn onto another street, assisted by the mirror that did exist on her side of the truck, and Chase's head whipped toward her as they approached Mason's auto garage, slowing to a stop near the open bay doors.

He sat up straight and said, "Whoa, whoa, whoa, whoa. Why are we stopping here?"

"Thanks for trying to arrange the other mechanic," she said, "but I had a better idea. I called up your dad. He said he'd help out if you did, too. Something about your million-dollar hands?"

"When did you call my dad?" he asked suspiciously. He didn't sound too mad—a little perturbed, maybe, but if pressed, she was sure that Chase would agree with her that Mason Taynor was the best mechanic for miles around.

"Right after you left to meet me at the dealership," she said. She tried to play innocent, but the look in Chase's eyes said he didn't buy her act. It was true that Mason had been part of her plan all along, and Jess had known that the short walk between the hardware store and the dealership would still allow her plenty of time to bring Chase's dad up to speed on her scheme.

She pulled up closer to the first open door and parked. Mason strolled out, walking toward the truck with his arms folded and a sly smile. Wes peeked out of the garage bay behind Mason, chocolate all over his face. At least, Jess hoped it was chocolate and not engine grease. Thanks to an in-service day at school, Wes had scored a long weekend, and once he'd known that Jess was set on buying the food truck, Jess couldn't have kept him at home if she'd tried.

She pulled the handle on the door, but it was stuck solid. Chase climbed down on his side and offered her a hand. Jess stepped out of the truck, steadying herself as her feet hit the pavement.

Jess called to Mason, "I brought you an assistant!"

"Hey, Dad." Chase stopped just short of the garage

bay. There was an awkward beat.

Mason unfolded his arms. In one of his hands was a pair of leather gloves. "These are for you," he said to Chase. "Ready to do some work, son?"

Wes, who had disappeared into Mason's office, now came barreling out with a clean face and launched himself at Chase and Jess. They both squeezed in together as Wes hugged them.

Chase, who caught the gloves as Mason tossed them, looked over at Jess and then down at Wesley. "Let's get started," he said to Mason.

Wes scampered back into the garage. Mason turned, Chase followed, and Jess took up the rear, pleased with what appeared to be the result of her swing for the fences—a solid base hit.

For the next several hours, they all worked as a team on the truck. She and Wes washed the outside of the grimy vehicle, soaping, scrubbing, and hosing off layers of dirt. Every so often, Jess would peek inside to see Chase and Mason scraping off old paint, installing a new faucet, rewiring the electrical—interspersed with sparse small talk that slowly grew into easy, lengthier conversation.

Jess remembered Chase being here at the garage, working many a summer during their time growing up in Parker Falls. It seemed that all Chase needed was to be reminded a little of that time—and of the man he'd spent that time with. And the same with Mason—Jess had seen the way he'd glared at Chase at the Spring Fling, and it had been clear to her that Chase's time away had made his father become the same—distant.

Lindy arrived with food and stayed for a bit, helping Wes finish scrubbing down the outside of the truck while Jessica and Chase cleared out the inside seats and wall paneling. Everyone said their goodbyes to Lindy as she loaded up her completely empty picnic basket and jetted off to play bridge.

Jess texted Nina to check on the diner, and Nina's reply had come with a reassurance that all was well—and a plethora of baseball emojis and kissing smiley faces. Jess ignored the kissing smiley faces. Her next text was to Brett, telling him that she had a surprise and asking him to meet her at the garage after he was done at the office. She'd avoided his calls lately. His first voicemail after their missed birthday date hadn't been a message reminding her that he would make it up to her, it had been an ecstatic announcement that he'd landed the Bacon Barrel franchise, and a lengthy explanation of how his new sales numbers compared to those of other insurance salesmen across the region.

They were all so into their restoration that the afternoon passed in a blink. Chase and Mason installed a new compact cooking range into the truck's interior. Jess started to protest when the expensive-looking appliance mysteriously appeared in the back of a lifted pickup truck, but Chase just waved her off.

"Didn't cost me a dime," Chase explained as Jess fretted over the range. "The guy wants tickets to see Boston at a spring training game. His mom lives in Florida, where we—*they* train. So let me leverage my remaining comp tickets while I still can. I'm certainly not showing my face there right now."

She relented. "Thank you. I feel like I keep saying that to you, but, really, thank you."

"You're welcome. Just a bad boy from Beantown, trying to win back some brownie points." He winked at her, and she was a little unnerved that the gesture was becoming so common—and that it made her feel so giddy. After the stove was in place, Jess hopped out of the truck and began picking up the tools that lay scattered around the garage floor.

Looking up from her work, she saw Wes watching a video on her phone. She hadn't even noticed that he'd snagged it.

"Whatcha watching, honey?" she asked.

"I filmed everything we did today. I think we can make a video showing people how we remade the truck, like on TV. That could help, right?"

Jess hadn't even thought about that. She held out her hand for her phone. "Great idea, sweetie! I'll take a look when we get home." He passed her the phone, and she glanced at her screen. There was a missed call and a text from Brett. He was on his way over to the garage. Chase rolled out from under the truck, startling her. Mason, who was just shutting the hood of the truck, came around and surveyed their work.

"We've still got a long way to go," Mason said. "But that's a good start. Not bad for a day's work."

Mason glanced over at Chase, who had emerged from beneath the truck covered in oil. He offered a hand to his son. Chase grabbed it and pulled up from the flat creeper dolly that he'd been sitting on.

"Looks like you got those million-dollar hands a little dirty," Mason joked.

Chase looked down at his hands. "I think it suits me just fine."

Jess watched them surreptitiously, pleased that the day had seemingly brought them close again. Mason clapped Chase on the back, and they headed into Mason's office. Just as Jess was putting the last tool in place on the cart, Brett pulled up. Wes screwed up his face as Brett got out of the car. Jess shot a look back at Wes, one that warned him to be nice.

"Hey, Jess, thanks for finally calling me back." Brett's annoyance was clear.

Jessica walked a few steps to meet Brett. "I know, I know. I'm sorry. I've just been busy," she said by way of explanation. She glanced over her shoulder at the truck and then smiled expectantly back at Brett, nervous about his reaction. She didn't want the positivity she'd felt all day to be doused by another lecture.

Brett's eyes widened, and his own smile was obviously forced. He said, "Don't tell me you bought a food truck." His expression was incredulous, as though he were talking to a client who'd just told him that they were switching insurance agents.

Brett stared at the truck and then back at Jessica. He didn't speak.

Jessica prompted, "What do you think?"

The silence grew uncomfortable as Brett seemed to search for something polite to say. Wes leaned on his elbows in the serving window, watching without shame. Jess winced. Thankfully, she was saved by Chase popping his head out of Mason's office.

"Hey, Jess!" he shouted and then, spotting Brett, said, "What's up, man?"

Brett's eyes narrowed slightly. He did not return Chase's greeting.

Chase continued, unabashed. "Dad's taking me back to the dealership to pick up my car. You guys all finished here? If not, can you lock up when you're done?"

Jess turned. "No, no, we can wrap up for the day. Tell your dad thanks again."

Chase gave a wave. "Will do."

As he disappeared, Wes came hopping down out of the truck. "Can we get pizza?" he asked Jess.

Brett uncharacteristically slung an arm around Wes.

"Sure, Wes, buddy," Brett replied. "I'll buy."

As Brett marched Wes toward the car, still resting a hand awkwardly on Wes's shoulder, Jess shook her head. Brett had managed to avoid talking about the truck while still inviting himself over to her house. The evening seemed like it was about to get tricky.

Chapter 13

*A*FTER THREE SLICES OF SUPREME pizza and a bath to rinse off layers of grease and grime that rivaled the old food truck, Wes fell asleep nearly instantly. After tucking Wes into bed, and without her son to act as a buffer between her and Brett, the subject of the truck couldn't be avoided. Jessica slipped back downstairs and sat down in the chair across from Brett, who was still at the dinner table. Jess's stomach had been in knots since they'd left the garage, and her pizza sat untouched on her plate.

He looked at her and smiled, but the gesture didn't reach his eyes. He gave the impression that he was waiting for her to start. He often waited for her to start conversations, and she wondered now if that was because he was always weighing the outcome of his own replies, never really risking saying the wrong thing—the emotional equivalent of an insurance policy. Brett was safe, that was true, but if he always played it safe, did she even have his heart?

Jessica said, "I guess I just thought you'd be happy for me."

"I *am* happy for you," he replied. "But we talked about this—the costs, the risks." Despite the fact that he must be hurt that Jess hadn't heeded his advice, his voice was gentle, even.

"And I appreciate your perspective," she assured him, "but this is something I really want to do."

"And the odds I explained to you?" he asked, spreading his hands in a futile gesture.

Jessica shot back, "Yes, there are going to be challenges, of course, but—"

Brett leaned across the kitchen table and clasped her hands in his, interrupting. "Jessica, Jessica. I'm only trying to keep you from making a mistake. Rolling the dice on a food truck, you could lose the diner!"

Jessica leaned in, too, fixing him with a serious stare. "And if I do nothing, and business doesn't get any better, then I'm going to lose the diner anyway."

Brett pulled back, sitting up straighter as he asserted, "You need to weigh the risks. It's just not worth it."

Jessica laughed, but it sounded hollow. It felt hollow. She couldn't believe that he was still clinging to his protests, that he refused to see her perspective on the whole thing, to see any merit in her just *trying*. "You are always trying to talk me out of these things!" she said, feeling her frustration rise.

Making light of her aggravation, Brett scoffed. "I'm just trying to help." He shook his head as if to clear it. "And who's been putting these ridiculous ideas into your head anyway?"

Jessica's mouth dropped open. The diner was hers, the responsibility hers, the dream of the food truck, the revamp of the menu, and the grand reopening—all of them were her ideas. Did Brett not think her capable of coming up with any of it by herself? And if not, did he think that she would be easily led into what he saw as a series of far-flung schemes that couldn't possibly succeed?

She found her voice, pushing aside her incredulity. "*I* have," she insisted. "You think my dreams are ridiculous?"

Brett swallowed and fell silent. Jess thought he was regretting saying what he honestly felt, rather than measuring his reply. It was probably about time he was a hundred percent honest. Jess was ready to be.

"I'm just giving you advice," Brett said, his careful voice returning. "And when you disregard it, maybe I feel like I'm wasting my time with you."

"Then maybe we both are," she fired back. She dropped her gaze to the table, gathering her own sense of calm. When she'd managed to, she said gently, "Look, you're a really great guy. But maybe we just need to take some time off."

Brett sighed, rubbing his hands on his pant legs as he rose from the table. "Yeah, maybe we do." He yanked his jacket off the back of his chair and didn't say anything else as he walked to the kitchen door.

He paused in the doorway.

"Y'know, Jess, Chase will be gone in a week. Think about the risk you'd be taking *there*."

She stared at him, her eyes going wide with surprise at his parting shot.

"Think about it," he repeated. Then he walked out, leaving her alone in her kitchen. She waited until the sound of his car engine faded before she put her head in her hands and let loose the tears she'd been holding back.

Chase felt sweat trickle down his temple and run down the side of his face. It was hot under the welder's mask, but he was nearly done fusing a new shelf under the serving window of the food truck.

The labor was a great distraction. After getting some bad news this morning that he was attempting to forget, Chase was determined to finish the truck's outside shelf today so he could move inside and add some similar shelving up near the ceiling to store extra paper supplies. The more he worked, the less he thought about all the things that might continue to fall apart from his old life.

In keeping with Jess's insistence that he not put any of his own money into the restoration of the truck, he'd gotten the heavy-gauge, diamond plate metal for the shelves from the town junkyard for nothing more than the time it had taken him to drive down and ask. He had ripped it from the remains of an old semi, and Chase had realized as he'd hauled the material out to his dad's truck that it felt remarkably good, using his hands for work that mattered to someone besides him. Sure, Chase had fans from his time in the league, but this was personal, deeper than any joy or disappointment at the outcome of a baseball game.

Mason had left Chase to work alone on the truck today, needing to catch up on his own customers. But father and son had labored side by side in neighboring bays, in a relative silence that wasn't uncomfortable anymore. Chase hadn't thanked Jess for pushing him and his father back together, but he hoped that his effort on the food truck was a fitting enough repayment. As the sparks flew from the welder's torch and Chase neared the end of the weld, he thought of Jess, anticipating her reaction to all the progress he'd made today.

"Hey. Wanna take a break?" Her voice came from

behind him. His dad appeared from around the back of the truck and shut off the welding torch at the source as Chase pushed up his heavy welder's mask. Jess and Wesley stood in the open bay door, watching Chase. Chase couldn't hold back his grin.

"I could use one, actually," he said, slicking his hair away from his damp forehead and walking out to take advantage of the breeze. Digging in her purse, Jess passed Wes a handful of change, and he high-fived Chase before sprinting down the sidewalk to the vending machine at the front of the garage.

Mason joined Chase and Jessica, greeting Jess before saying to Chase, "Hey, I checked your work under the hood."

Chase braced for the return of his dad's crotchety mood and critical comments. He wouldn't relish the criticism, but if Mason had noticed anything off, Chase wanted to hear it. He didn't want any lingering problems with the truck for Jess.

"Okay, Dad, let me have it," he said.

Mason paused for a moment, looking at the weld Chase had made. "Your welding work's not half bad."

"Really?" Chase was surprised. Maybe his dad was buttering him up with a compliment only to drop the hammer with a long list of negatives about the repairs Chase had done on the cooling system in the truck.

Mason asked, "You used my old spray bottle trick, didn't ya?" There was a ghost of a smile starting up at the corner of his mouth.

Chase narrowed his eyes and nodded slowly. "Yeah, Dad, of course."

Jessica, who watched their exchange with a look of trepidation on her face, said, "What's the spray bottle trick?"

Chase explained, "Spraying water on the belt to make sure that the noise it made all the way here isn't a bad water pump."

Jessica socked Mason good-naturedly on the shoulder. "Looks like you taught your son a bit."

Mason chuckled and rolled his eyes. "Yeah, when he listened."

Wes ran up with an armful of cold sodas. As he passed them around, he informed Mason, "Chase says you taught him a lot of things. You taught him his first curveball."

"Thanks, bud," Chase said, accepting a drink from Wes and ruffling his hair.

Mason popped the tab on his soda and glanced over at Chase. "I'm surprised you remember that."

"You bet I do." Chase toasted his dad with his grape soda. He nodded toward Wesley. "A good friend jogged my memory."

The sound of tires crunching gravel sounded, and Chase's mom pulled up. Chase jogged out to meet her and opened her car door.

"Oh!" Chase heard Jess say suddenly. "Wes, can you go back to the car and get the brushes and smocks?" Chase gave a hand to Lindy as she climbed out of her car. The two of them made it back to the bay just as Wes returned with the supplies.

"Paint's in the office," Mason said to his wife, as she leaned in and kissed his cheek. "I'm going home to shower."

"Good," Lindy said, wrinkling her nose. "You smell like a mechanic."

Chase's heart warmed as he watched his parents hug tightly. Despite their good-natured bickering, it had been a blessing to grow up with two people who also happened to be each other's best friends. Wes offered Lindy a smock, and she accepted it. Then she looked at Chase and Jessica.

"Okay, shoo, you two! Wesley and I are gonna do some painting, and we artists need our creative space!" Wes nodded, doing his best to appear haughty.

Jessica glanced at Chase. "You hungry?"

"Starving. All day at a food truck, and no food in sight. Spring Fling's still going, and it has everything a growing boy needs." Junk food sounded perfect to him after today's grueling work.

Jess's phone rang. Chase, standing next to her, couldn't help but notice the name that flashed on the screen. He averted his eyes and was prepared to wait for her to take her phone call from Brett, but she hit ignore and pocketed the phone. *Interesting.*

Jess looked from Wes to Chase and, smiling, said, "Suits me fine. We'll be back in a couple hours, okay?"

Wes hugged his mom and then Chase, and when Wes and Lindy went off chattering into the office to retrieve their paint, Chase nodded toward his dad's truck. "Let me catch a ride to my parents' first. Mom may have been ribbing Dad, but I honestly *do* smell like a mechanic."

They ate a lunch at the Spring Fling that no mom would have approved of, which consisted of nachos, hot dogs, and a monster turkey leg that Jess watched Chase eat with a true sense of astonishment. Afterward, Jessica sat at a table with Chase in the center of the festivities, both of them downing ice-cream sundaes as people strolled through the community center.

Chase finished off the last bite of his triple scoop and sat back. Jess was sure that her face must have been registering turkey-leg-level disbelief because he grinned and said, "Nothing compares to the local ice cream here. And you know, technically, I'm still in training."

Jessica said, "It's fine by me. This table is a judgment-free zone. I'm drowning my sorrows in sugar today. Exercise that arm by lifting a few more scoops." She pushed her empty cup toward him, which had held its fair share before she'd dug in.

"Jess," Chase said and then hesitated. She looked quizzically at him, and he continued. "I'm sorry about you and Brett."

Jess had the strangest feeling that what he'd said wasn't what he'd *wanted* to say. She felt her lips draw into a tight line. "Don't be. So I didn't take his advice? If that's too much for him to handle, then we weren't as close as I thought to begin with."

Chase hesitated and then admitted, "That…well, I guess that makes two of us."

Uh-oh. Jess watched as Chase pulled out his cell phone and clicked a few times. "What do you mean?" she asked.

Chase handed her his phone. On the screen was a photo from a tabloid newspaper. The headline emblazoned over the image of a bikini-clad Heather frolicking with a man who definitely wasn't Chase read:

Taynor Loses Again! First the Game, Now the Girl!

"Ouch," Jess said simply. "What happened?"

Chase said, "I saw this online this morning. Picture of Heather on my old teammate's yacht. I guess she went from Paris to Miami." His tone was light, but she knew that the breakup had to be a blow. One on top of another, she guessed, especially since he hadn't mentioned anything about a sudden resolution to his still-looming career troubles.

Jessica studied the photo. "Yeah, they look a little too friendly to be friends," she commiserated.

"It explains why she hasn't been returning my texts."

Jess handed back his phone, and he cast a last stormy scowl at the photo before shutting off the screen and shoving the device back into his pocket. He sighed. "I guess she wants to be on the winning team."

Jessica knew exactly how he was feeling. Well, not *exactly*. While she and Brett hadn't been ideal for each other, Brett had at least been a faithful guy. It was awful that Heather hadn't even had the manners to break up with Chase honestly. If everyone that Chase had been surrounded by in Boston was like her, no wonder he felt so out-of-touch with the real world, with good people—people who truly cared for him.

"Chase, I'm really sorry," she said, reaching out to cover his hand with hers.

"I'd also guess her visit's off." He paused for a moment, eyeing the table, which was still covered in the empty plastic baskets, crumpled napkins, and various other detritus from their fair food marathon. "But something tells me that she wouldn't have enjoyed it much here anyway."

They both couldn't help but laugh.

"Yeah," Jess said, feeling a little better as she giggled. "Probably not."

Chase picked up his spoon and licked it. "Probably not." He wagged his eyebrows at Jess. They were being silly, but more and more, Jess was seeing the Chase she remembered come back, the Chase who didn't care if he was acting like a total fool as long as she was laughing with him.

Jessica said, "You know, we have a couple of hours. Maybe we could both use a change of scenery."

Chase wasn't sure what she had in mind, but he nodded. "Lead the way."

The drive to Jessica's suggested change of scenery was very familiar to Chase. He kept his reaction under wraps, but his heart was beating a little faster as they parked and walked to duck into the canopy of the forest. This part of the woods was state land, and though the public could access it freely, when they'd been in high school, it hadn't been that popular because it had been harder to get to than it was now. Back then, the wide, well-kept gravel parking area hadn't existed, and he and Jess had parked his old Ford just off the main highway and walked to the trailhead.

Once they were a few paces down the trail, Chase inhaled a deep breath of the cool, sparkling air. Man, this took him right back. "Wow. I remember this path."

"I hope so," Jess said. "We used to come here almost every week after school."

Chase studied her out of the corners of his eyes. "Yeah, we'd hide underneath the trees, and I'd try to steal a kiss."

She gave him a playful push on the shoulder. He grinned back at her.

"You'd plan your escape from this town," she reminded him.

Chase stopped near the edge of the creek. It was almost as if his feet had known the number of steps to the bank. Looking back as Jess drew up beside him, he shook his head.

"*Our* escape," he corrected. He hadn't wanted to leave Jess in Parker Falls. She had been afraid to come with him, and he hadn't understood why. He'd reacted, she'd reacted, and the whole immature mess had driven them apart for fifteen years.

"Yeah, I know," she said softly. Her eyes held his for a few seconds, and he wondered how she would react if he tried to steal a kiss now. She broke their gaze, and he stared out over the creek. This felt so *right*, being back in Parker Falls, spending time with Jess. But with both of them newly single, and with all the emotional history in this place, Chase wondered about the wisdom of coming out here. Were they setting themselves up for more heartache?

Jessica, as if reading his thoughts, said, "This town always gave me a reason to stay. First, Grandpa and then my parents."

Chase turned his back on the creek, facing Jess and watching her intently as she stared out over the water. These fifteen years had given her as many challenges as it had given him privileges, and as she started to reflect on them, he felt a sadness sweep over him at the slight bitterness on her beautiful face.

"Then I stayed for Davis." She pressed her lips together, and he thought again, crazily, about kissing her, if only to erase the pain from her face.

She looked over at him. "I think, deep down, I was just scared."

Chase cleared his throat, tried to sound breezier than he felt. "It happens to the best of us."

He scanned the woods again. His attention caught on a tree behind her.

"No way."

He paused in amazement. Jess turned to follow his line of sight and gasped in surprise. Chase covered the few yards between them and the tree with Jess close behind him.

"I can't believe this is still here," he said, reaching out to trace the faded inscription on the trunk. "Remember when I carved that?" He marveled that his handiwork had survived all these years.

Jess examined the tree trunk, her face filled with wonder. "'J & C forever'? That was a little overly optimistic," she teased.

Chase heard the words slip out before he could even think about them. "Well, maybe the game's not over yet." As soon as he said it, his chest seized with a burst of uncertainty. When she didn't respond, he turned to find her wide-eyed and standing closer than he'd expected.

Neither of them spoke. The wind blew through the trees, carrying with it the exact same sounds and scents that it had all those years ago. He leaned closer. She didn't pull back.

Her lashes fluttered downward, and Chase's heart raced at breakneck speed. Would this be considered stealing a kiss? Everything about her was telling him she would welcome the touch of his lips on hers.

Jessica's phone dinged. Startled, she scrambled to dig it out of her pocket, breaking the spell of the moment. "H—hold on. Sorry," she stammered.

Chase turned away as she checked her messages. He scrubbed a hand over his face.

What are you thinking, Taynor?

Jessica said, "It's your mom. They're all done painting the truck."

"Okay," he said, knowing that his voice sounded rough

and unsteady. The flush in her cheeks told him that she felt the same—knocked off her axis. Chase offered her a hand as they started up the hill to the trailhead, and Jess accepted it. As they picked their way back through the forest to the parking lot, he was thrilled that their fingers stayed entwined.

Chapter 14

$\mathscr{T}$HE TRUCK SAT PARKED IN the late afternoon sun, and Lindy had departed a few minutes earlier as Chase, Jessica, and Wesley stood in front of the garage and marveled at the new paint job. The cheerful green-and-white color scheme made the vehicle look fresh and inviting, and the words emblazoned across the side read "Wesley's On Wheels" and "Bringing Your Hometown Diner Right to You" over a dancing array of crisply stenciled diner foods.

Wesley beamed up at Chase and said, "Isn't it great?"

Jessica's eyes were fixed on Chase and Wes as they stood next to each other, and she had to force herself to look back at the truck. After what had almost happened in the woods, she was seriously conflicted about how much time she and Wesley might be spending with Chase between now and when Chase eventually—no, when he *inevitably*—left.

Chase said, "Buddy, it's fantastic. A real work of art!" He hugged Wes close to him, and Jess's reservations crumbled. Even if Chase was gone in a week, as Brett had warned, she could have this time. She could keep it as a good memory, not as a sad reminder of what she—what *they*—might have had.

Jessica surveyed the truck again. She was astonished. She couldn't believe what Lindy and Wes had done with just supplies from the hardware store. "Your mom is a phenomenal artist. It's unreal. Now, Lindy says that even though the paint she used is quick-dry, there's still the clear coat to put on tomorrow. And the kitchen is still a work in progress. But I say we load it up with stuff from the diner and take this baby out for a test run! Maybe even field-test some new menu items?"

Chase nodded, getting into the notion. "That's a great idea."

"Yeah?" Jess asked. It was nice, how willing Chase was to be involved, how supportive he was of her ambitions. The more time she spent with him, the less she felt that she was just small-town, the less she felt held back by fear of the unknown. Whatever happened in the future, Chase or no Chase, he had at least pushed her past her misgivings. He had given her the gift of believing in herself.

"Where do you think should be our first stop?" he asked her.

Jessica thought back to the last place she'd eaten a memorable meal and let a daring smile curl her lips. "I know just the place."

The evening air was as brisk as the business they were doing from the truck. Out from the new striped awning, a line of customers stretched, vying for position in front of the truck's open serving window. Chase manned the grill. Wes buzzed around with Jess's phone in hand, taking pictures and short videos and posting them to a slew of new social media profiles that he and Jess had set up for the new "Wesley's On Wheels". Jess leaned out to hear her next customer over the sound of the carnival rides just behind the line, soaking in the energy of the Spring Fling.

The woman, raising her own voice to be heard, shouted merrily, "An empanada, please."

"Okay! Hey, guys," Jess called over her shoulder to Chase and Wesley. Wes hung out the window beside Jess and handed over a Styrofoam container while the woman passed Jess the cash to pay for the food. Jess tapped the bills jauntily on the edge of the serving counter, smiling at the woman. "There's more where that came from," Jess chirped. She couldn't help herself. Her optimism was soaring high.

"Oh," the woman said, looking over the whiteboard menu that leaned against the truck. "I'll have three corn dogs, then, please."

Wes was already on it as Jess spun and said, "Oh! Three corn dogs?"

Jess was thrilled to see that her new menu items were selling. The jalapeno-bacon corn dogs had been made from scratch back at the diner. She'd used stadium-sized hot dogs and adapted the batter with some of her favorite ingredients. With a whipped honey dip on the side, they were flying out the window. She made a mental note to experiment with a maple-bacon version.

Another customer crowded up. Jess smiled down at him, ready to take his order. Her gaze flicked up and over the gathered crowd while she waited to hear his selection. She was slightly dismayed to see Charlie appear at the back of the line, studying the truck and the big crowd that swarmed it. She shook off her distaste.

Good. Let him look. Maybe he'll pick up a few pointers from his new competition.

The man Jess had smiled at spoke up. "Is that Chase Taynor serving burgers?" he asked.

"It is," Jess confirmed, glad to hear Chase laugh behind her.

"Would you be willing to autograph my hamburger in mustard?" he called to Chase.

"He will, yes," Jess agreed before Chase could even make it to the window.

"Well, there's a first time for everything, right?" Chase asked.

The woman who'd requested the corn dogs was passed her order, and there was a wave of laughter from the crowd as Chase picked up the mustard dispenser and scribbled onto a burger that Wes set in front of him.

"Oh," Jess said to Chase, impressed. "Fancy!" Chase put a little spin on the mustard bottle and slid it six-shooter style back into the condiment caddy.

"Enjoy!" Chase said as he closed the takeout container and handed off the sandwich. He turned and gave Jess a playful hip bump before returning to the grill. Wes, at the counter next to Chase, busied himself packing soda cans down into a deep stainless reservoir filled with ice.

Jessica sorted the money from the last two customers into her cash box and realized that things were going so well on their maiden run that she'd have enough to make the first payment on the truck just from tonight's profits. She closed the lid of the box and lifted her head to see Charlie standing in front of the window.

Must have elbowed his way to the front. That seems about right.

Charlie was holding a cone of bright blue cotton candy, but if he thought that it made him blend in with the crowd, he was so, so wrong. With his slicked-back hair and expensive suit, he appeared completely out of place in the casual crowd.

"What is this?" he asked, a sneer on his face as the question rolled out in his New York accent. Jess felt Chase's hand at her waist. She looked back over her shoulder at him. Chase shot her a brief, concerned look, but she just shook her head.

"I'm fine," she mouthed.

Spinning to see that Charlie's arrogant expression hadn't changed, she said as brightly as she could, "Well, hello, Charlie."

"A rolling diner with a celebrity chef? Really?"

Jess wasn't fazed by him. She had a strong inkling that he'd come down to the Spring Fling just to check out what she was up to. After all, even though his restaurant sponsored some of the Spring Fling events, Charlie wasn't anywhere close to being a small-town, homespun event kind of a guy. And Parker Falls was a very small town—one that loved to talk. If Charlie had taken time out to leave his restaurant to attend an event he normally wouldn't be caught dead at, that meant that they'd rattled him a little. She hoped *that* little tidbit made it into the gossip rounds.

Jess played a bit dumb, pursing her lips and letting her head fall to one side. "But didn't you say a little competition raises the bar for everyone?"

Charlie sputtered. Jess wondered how the taste of his own words, now that he was eating them, compared to the cotton candy in his hand.

Wesley leaned on his elbows in the serving window. "Would you like a corn dog, sir?" he asked Charlie, signature mischievous smile firmly in place.

Charlie stared at Wesley, blustering, "No, I wouldn't like a corn dog, thank you." He turned and walked away, mumbling to himself. "Humph. Celebrity chef?"

Jess felt Chase brush against her as he handed the last of the orders out the window. He didn't pull away immediately, instead leaning in and whispering to her, "Good job, slugger. That guy seemed a little lofty to me."

His voice in her ear made the hairs on the back of her neck stand up. She thought back to the look in his eyes when they'd almost kissed in the woods, to the way he'd leaned close.

"Do you ever cater?" The question broke into Jess's thoughts. It came from the woman who'd bought three of Jess's corn dogs. "My company picnic's coming up," the woman explained, holding out a business card.

Jessica took the card, exclaiming, "Yes! We do! And also, we love seeing old friends back at Wesley's diner." Jessica spoke up, projecting to all the waiting customers. "In fact, the grand reopening is coming up, and we're debuting new items on the menu. So, everyone, please come, and tell all of your friends. Thank you so much!"

The crowd was murmuring, and the next couple in line stepped forward. Jessica turned to Chase. He tipped a thumb toward the empty chafing dishes and the empty meat cooler.

Jess realized what he was saying. She'd never been happier about running out of supplies.

"We're all out?" she asked.

Chase nodded, and Jess pulled them all into a huddle. "Let's go back to the diner, we'll restock, and then we'll take a trip around town. Yeah?"

Chase said, "Okay. Sounds great." Wes, who Jess knew was as happy as a pig in mud due to being able to avoid his math homework, added his own enthusiastic agreement. He high-fived his mom. Chase and Jess high-fived. It was cheesy, all the high-fiving, but Jess felt like she could slap palms with the entire crowd that still stood outside the serving window.

"Thanks, guys," Chase called to the crowd who began to disperse. Some of them pulled out their phones and took pictures of Chase, Jess, and Wes standing there, waving.

"Thank you!" Jess repeated, bouncing on her heels with glee. As Wes updated their schedule online and posted the route that Jess had told him the truck would take around Parker Falls, Jess and Chase began to pack up.

They closed the truck's awning and rolled onward.

"Thanks for the inaugural ride in Wesley's On Wheels," Chase said as he stepped out of Jess's car later that evening, leaning over to look through the passenger's window. She nodded, and her eyes flicked to something behind him. Glancing over his shoulder, Chase spotted Mason sitting on the front porch of the Taynors' house. Mason gave a wave, which Jess and Wesley returned, and Chase got a funny twist in his stomach. He still worried that, despite the seeming reconciliation between Mason and him, conflict was just below the surface, ready to spring up. Chase was reminded that he hadn't thanked Jess for her plan to get him reconnected with his father, not in any verbal way.

"And thanks for helping me mend some fences with my dad."

"It's the least I could do. You've been a huge help with Wes, with the truck. It's been nice having you back."

Her choice of words made the twist in his gut wind even tighter. This time, it wasn't with trepidation, but with some deep longing that he didn't care to explore right now. Not with his dad watching them. He felt like a teenager.

He nodded to her and said to Wes, "See you later, bud."

"Bye!" Wes replied, grinning that grin that always got Chase to smile back. Chase thumped the car door lightly as he pushed away to head to the house.

She called out through the open window, "Bye! And don't forget, the auction's tomorrow!"

Chase yelled back, "Right, meet you there!"

Chase jogged up the porch steps, avoiding his father's odd little knowing look, hoping that they wouldn't have to talk about how much time Chase had been spending with Jess and Wesley. Despite the sparkle in his dad's eye that told Chase that the elder Taynor wanted to grill him right off the bat, thankfully, it wasn't the first thing that Mason brought up.

"Hey, Chase, look what your mother found," Mason said, pointing to a stack of scrapbooks that occupied the bistro table on the porch.

Chase sat down in the chair opposite his father and picked up one of the big scrapbooks, flipping it open to see it filled with faded newspaper clippings.

Chase tapped a yellowed article. "Wow, this is from my junior high school paper."

Mason said, "You took the team all the way to state that year." Mason reached over and browsed through a few pages as if he knew the order of the books by heart. He found what he was looking for. "And that is the first time you were mentioned in a real newspaper."

Chase was flabbergasted. "Hey, that's when I signed my first contract."

Mason nodded, moving his finger over the other items on the page. "The tickets stubs, everything's there from your first game."

Something was slowly dawning on Chase. His whole career, he'd not come home to Parker Falls to see his parents regularly—but that didn't mean that they'd never come to Boston to see him. "I didn't know you were there. Why didn't you tell me?"

Mason admitted, somewhat sheepishly, "We didn't want to throw you off on your big day."

Chase paged through the scrapbook. The clippings weren't pasted neatly. There were no fancy borders or crafty embellishments. His mother hadn't put these books together—these things had all been saved by his dad. "Why haven't you shown me this before now?"

Mason said, "Well, your mom always puffed you up so much, I figured it was my job to keep you grounded."

Chase felt a disbelieving laugh escape him as he picked up a second book and began to flip through it. The amount of care that his father had taken to chronicle Chase's career was touching and unexpected.

"I don't wear my heart on my sleeve," Mason continued, giving Chase a sincere look. "But I've always been proud of you. You chased your dreams."

"Thanks, Dad," Chase said quietly.

"So what's really bothering you, son?"

Chase swiped a hand over his mouth. It wasn't easy for him, being open with his father. But since returning to Parker Falls, Chase was beginning to see that the past was a place he might not want to dwell in—or run from—anymore.

"I guess I…I just don't know what to hope for these days. I've spent fifteen years building my career, and lately, I've been afraid to check my messages 'cause I don't know what I want to hear."

Mason said, "Afraid? That's not a word we hear much from you." Mason paused for a moment. "You always made your dreams happen. Don't give up on them now." Mason gave Chase a meaningful look. "Whatever they are."

Chase said, "Thanks, Dad. And not just for all the help this week. For everything, always. I definitely owe you more than one."

Mason said, "Nothing to owe. And as for the help on the truck, I always liked Jessica. Truth is, I always hoped you two would somehow end up back together. Didn't seem in the cards, though. This little town was always too small to hold you."

"Oh yeah?" That was surprising. When Chase and Jess had dated, his father used to joke good-naturedly with Chase about how Lindy was planning Chase and Jessica's wedding. Chase's mother hadn't missed the opportunity to regale her son with his old flame's life story once she knew he was headed home. But his father hadn't mentioned Jess once in the years since Chase had left Parker Falls.

"Maybe it took finally coming back here to realize I've missed this place. That I've missed the *people* that are this place." Chase scanned over his parents' lush green lawn. Beside the big oak in the front yard, he noticed his mother standing half-hidden behind an easel. She peeked out at them and then ducked quickly behind her canvas. Chase could see the end of her paintbrush twitching.

Chase cast a glance at his dad. "Um, Dad, is Mom

painting us over there?"

Mason said, "Yes, she is." He sighed. "Best thing to do is just smile."

Chase's face split into a grin. He hoped that in his mother's newest painting, his dad was the hero.

Chapter 15

*W*EDNESDAY FLEW BY ALMOST AS fast as the day they'd started overhauling the food truck. There was a slight uptick in business at the diner, which Jess attributed to their spin in the "WOW"—the nickname Wes had given Wesley's On Wheels. After a fair breakfast and lunch rush, Jess spent the afternoon trying to drum up more items for the Spring Fling auction.

Despite her efforts—and her reminder to every business she called that the sale was being held as a benefit for Wes's elementary school—the offerings she had secured weren't likely to bring in any big bucks. Disappointed, Jess had shot a last-minute text to Chase, asking if he could donate some memorabilia. He'd agreed, giving Jess one more thing to thank him for.

After her obligatory phone calls, she'd paid the first payment on the truck out of her profits from the WOW and taken care of a few outstanding invoices from her food vendors. She crossed the two debts off her list of bills. Though both of her financial accomplishments made her proud, her list still reminded her that she had to make the payment on her loan, fast. Maybe she should have put the truck money to the loan, but she'd rationalized that even if she lost the diner, she could still swing the truck payment. She could use the truck to begin again. It was exactly where her grandfather had started, and Jess would feel no shame in it at all.

The diner stayed slow through dinner, and Jess used the time to work on the new menu. Wes's babysitter dropped him off just after the last patron had left, and Nina and Jess locked up a little early to head to the auction. Jess still hadn't heard from Chase, so she shot him a quick reminder text to meet them at the community center. Her phone dinged seconds later with his response.

See you there.

But Jess didn't see Chase there, and she had flashbacks to Brett's flakiness as the night's festivities started up. The event was presided over by Mayor Fletcher, who called out to the bidders from a podium on the stage. Jessica and Nina watched from the midst of the crowd as Wesley played a ring toss game with some of his baseball teammates.

Not only were there not that many items to offer, but interest wasn't high, despite how the whole town of Parker Falls seemed to have assembled at the Fling tonight. Crowds milled, and there was even a significant audience gathered, some on folding chairs, some standing around the main stage.

Jess fidgeted as items came and went and the auction drew nearer to its close. She'd hoped that the event would be a good fundraiser for the elementary school and allow for some new computer equipment the classrooms sorely needed, but the overall funds raised weren't enough, and items still left to come up on the block were few and measly. Jess bit a fingernail as the mayor shuffled some papers and leaned toward the microphone.

"Just a quick announcement before we continue with the auction. Congratulations to Becky's Best Pies, winner of this year's pie contest!"

Jess frowned, her mood dipping a little further. Great. She'd even lost the pie contest. That was no cherry-guava surprise, the way her luck was turning out today. Her phone dinged, and she glanced down to see a text from Chase.

I'm here.

Her mood instantly rebounded. Jess looked up to see Nina grinning at her.

"What?" Jess said.

Her friend just grinned wider. "Text from Chase?"

Jess avoided answering, pointing to the podium where the mayor was starting up the bidding again.

Nina threw up her hands. "Oh, please. The whole town knows you guys are like bread and butter again. Just get together already!" Nina indicated a group of ladies who stood nearby. "The rest of the PTA has a pool on when the first kiss is going to happen."

Jess felt her face flush at the idea. Not of the PTA pool—Parker Falls was notoriously nosy, though well-meaning—but at the thought of a first kiss with Chase. *Another* first kiss.

Mayor Fletcher turned up his microphone a bit and boomed out over the crowd, trying to entice anyone not in the audience to come watch the rest of the proceedings. "Okay, everyone, it's time for tonight's big auction. C'mon, folks, it's for the school, and I see a lot of bad haircuts out there! So, do I hear forty dollars for a deluxe styling from Betty's Hair Salon?"

An old lady shouted, "Ten dollars!" The mayor waited for a beat, and then another. No other bidders chimed in. Jess winced. If this was any indication of how the remaining bidding would go, the kids would be drawing on cardboard boxes and using their imaginations for their classroom tech.

The mayor looked around for another bidder. Still, no one spoke up.

Reluctantly, the mayor said, "Going once, going twice. Sold!"

There was light clapping. Jessica whispered over to Nina. "Ugh. Not exactly raising a mint here. The bids are almost over."

Jess heard a familiar voice murmuring at the edge of the crowd, and Chase approached, excusing himself as he squeezed past every person between that edge and Jessica. He was carrying a cardboard box and wearing a tight, long-sleeved sweater that Jess couldn't help but appreciate.

Nina elbowed Jess and said, "There he is." There was another knowing look, this time one that Jess saw Nina give to the PTA group. The other ladies responded with none-too-subtle winks and looks of their own.

If I roll my eyes anymore, Jess thought, *they might just pop out of my head.* She was relieved when Chase made it over.

"Hey," Jess said, peering into the box. The gaggle of staring moms tittered in unison. She ignored them.

"Sorry I'm late," he said. He began rifling through the items he'd gathered. "I didn't know what to bring, so I just brought some options. What were you thinking for the auction? I got signed baseballs, a jersey, I think I have a glove in there, as well. Whatever you guys need."

Jess smiled slyly. "Really? Anything?"

Chase's attention bounced from Jess to Nina and back again. His expression said that he had no idea what Jess was about to drop on him. Beside her, Nina grinned. They'd bandied the idea around before Chase had arrived, but Jess hadn't been confident that their idea would be successful until now. Inspired by the cut of his sweater, she was now pretty darned confident. Surely, she wasn't the only female with an appreciative eye in the crowd.

"Well, what are you thinking?" he asked uncertainly.

Jessica said, "Well, we had an idea of how you could help." Impulsively, Jess rose on tiptoe and hooked a hand behind his neck, drawing him down so she could whisper in his ear. "We could auction *you* off."

Chase drew back, laughing, his eyes darting between the two women again, seemingly waiting for the punch-line. "You're joking!"

Nina and Jess shook their heads in sync, both smiling hopefully. He stared at Jess, and she could almost see the wheels turning as he mulled the idea over and then caved. He shook his head. "I guess it's for a good cause."

"Thank you!" Jess chirped, not waiting for him to change his mind. She bounced through the crowd and up on stage, followed by the sound of Nina's gleeful clapping. Jessica made it up to the podium and whispered to the mayor, who began chuckling but nodded.

Mayor Fletcher turned to the crowd. Jess stayed on stage to make sure that Chase didn't bolt if he was promised to a zealous octogenarian with a twenty-dollar bill and wandering hands.

"Please bring the next item to the podium," Mayor Fletcher called.

"That's you," Nina said to Chase, loudly enough to be heard over the now-cheering onlookers. The same woman who'd scored the hair styling prize whooped and checked Chase out as he passed her. Jess could see that he was blushing as he was herded up to stand between the mayor and Jessica. He shook hands with the mayor and then stood at attention in a pose he probably thought looked studly, but Jess likened more to a Ken doll still in the box.

She elbowed him gently. "Loosen up," she whispered.

The mayor said, "Our final item for auction is Parker Falls' most famous former resident. Sure, he's got a few dings." Fletcher socked Chase on the arm, and Chase hammed it up, patting his other shoulder and wincing as if it were lame. The mayor continued. "But he shines up okay. So, what's the first bid for a dance date with our hometown hero?"

The same old lady who'd won the haircut called out, "Twenty dollars!"

Chase's face registered surprise—or was that mild fear? Jess nearly burst out laughing.

A striking, well-dressed, older woman chimed in. "Fifty dollars!" Chase's eyes cut over to the other woman. He looked relieved that she didn't have blue hair, and then a little interested. Jess felt the tiniest flare of jealousy come out of nowhere.

The mayor said, "Do I hear a hundred?"

The old lady shouted, "A hundred dollars!" The crowd collectively turned their heads to gape at her.

The well-dressed woman yelled, "One twenty!"

The old lady raised again. "One forty!" At this point, Jess was getting whiplash, along with the rest of the crowd, as heads seesawed back and forth between the rival bidders. Jess saw Nina shuffle over to the PTA group and lean in to whisper with them.

The mayor turned his eyes to the well-dressed woman, who glared at the other bidder but remained silent. The old woman's face was gleeful. Chase had the look of a deer in the headlights. Seeing no other bids, the mayor said, "One forty, going once, going twice—"

Nina caught Jess's eye. One of the PTA women leaned over and said something hurriedly to Nina that Jess couldn't make out. Nina threw up a hand, her index finger raised.

Nina shouted to the mayor. "Can we bid as a group?"

Jess frowned at Nina, unsure of what her friend and the gaggle of women were about to do, and then glanced over at Chase, who shrugged.

The mayor considered it a moment. "I don't see why not."

Nina grinned and consulted with the flock. "Three hundred and twelve dollars!" she shouted after they'd conferred.

Mayor Fletcher looked delighted. "Three hundred and twelve dollars, going once, twice, sold!"

The old woman shook her head, grumbling at losing her prize. Nina raised a fist in victory. The crowd cheered. Jessica watched the group of women—whose scheme she still didn't quite understand—hug and congratulate each other. When the noise settled, Jess felt the eyes of every PTA member looking at her and Chase.

Chase leaned over and whispered to Jessica. "I don't know if I like the looks of this."

"Me neither," Jess agreed.

They descended the steps from the stage and Nina rushed up with Wes by her side and the PTA in full force behind. Nina handed the box of Chase's sports memorabilia to Wes and gripped Jess's shoulders.

"Forgive us. We do this out of love," Nina said. Jess still wasn't sure what was happening, but she was now *certain* that the mom squad and Nina had cooked up something Jess was bound to be mortified by. Nina was up on stage in a flash, and the mayor was leaning over to be whispered to again. Mayor Fletcher laughed heartily, stepped aside, and gestured for Nina to take the microphone.

"Hey, Parker Falls!" Nina said loudly—too loudly. The microphone in front of her whined with ear-splitting feedback. Chase made a face, and Jess plugged her ears. Maybe I should keep them plugged, she thought.

Nina pulled the mic away and tried again. "We, as a group, have decided that our auction prize of a dance date with Chase Taynor should be given to Jessica Parker."

Jessica's eyes flew wide as the crowd cheered again. She started to shake her head, but then she felt Chase's fingers slip through hers. When she peeked over, she discovered that his blush had returned. She was sure she looked just as embarrassed, judging by the heat in her cheeks.

The PTA moms shooed at them. Chase tugged her hand, and Jessica followed him out past the lingering crowd to the center of the floor near the back of the room, which had been cleared to form a temporary dance floor.

Jessica said, "I'm not sure how I feel about this."

"At least it's for a good cause," Chase reassured her.

Up on stage, the mayor exited, and a local band that was set up on a side stage began to play a slow, sultry tune.

"Really, I shouldn't be surprised. This town always gets in everyone's business," Jess groused, though there was no malice in her statement. She felt secretly thrilled that Nina and the mom squad had meddled. What she was uncertain about was how *Chase* felt about it.

"Just so half the town doesn't feel cheated, any chance you want to dance?" Chase asked lightly.

Jess realized with a start that he was choosing his

words carefully because *he* wasn't sure how *she'd* react. How funny, both of them dancing around, well, dancing.

Jessica paused and then spun to hold out her other hand to him. "Let's dance," she said.

Chase smiled, his eyes alight with pleasure as he pulled her in close. One of his arms slid around her waist. She stepped in, and her cheek rested in the crook of his neck. They began to sway to the music, Chase leading. Just before Jess relaxed in his arms and closed her eyes, she saw Wesley and Nina watching them from the edges of the crowd. She threw a warm smile their way. Chase gave Wesley a nod, and Wesley broke into a big grin.

As Jess hooked a hand over Chase's shoulder and sighed, Chase said, "This takes me back."

"The lights, the music…" She searched for what to say next, not trusting herself to keep her true feelings under wraps in this perfect moment.

Chase finished, "And you." He pulled away to look into her eyes. Her heart hammered in her chest, and she couldn't hold back. She'd taken risks since Chase had come home, risks that had paid off. But she'd never know if this one would unless she went for it.

Jessica stared into the beautiful blue eyes that she'd fallen in love with all those years ago. "Maybe you can go home again," she said, hoping that he wouldn't pull away, shutting her out and reminding her that he was on his way back to some big city the second after the ink dried on a new baseball contract.

He didn't pull away. He didn't say a word. The electric guitar that backed the slow song twanged, low and sensual, as Chase's arm tightened around her. She held her breath. Seconds later, beneath the twinkling fairy lights strung from the ceiling, Chase and Jessica kissed.

Chapter 16

THE BANNER FLAPPING ACROSS THE awning of Wesley's said Grand Reopening Tonight! Jess stood outside in the spring sunshine, staring up at the words with a distracted smile on her face. She looked at the diner, but she thought about Chase— the way he'd held her as they danced, the look in his eyes when she'd leaned into him, and that kiss.

Nina popped out of the front door of the diner. She was tying on a clean apron as she shouted to Jess. "Come on! Let's get ready for our grand reopening!"

Jess shook off her daydream, but she couldn't shake off—didn't want to shake off—the feeling of joy and utter contentment that flooded her when she stepped back into the diner. She stood in the doorway and watched the bustle of activity for a moment. Cal and Chase were clearing tables out of the dining room, and Nina was instructing Wes on the responsible use of a full spray bottle of window cleaner. Someone had started up the jukebox, and upbeat music flowed into the room.

Nina spotted Jess. "Hey, don't just stand there!"

Chase glanced up from his work and fixed her with

a warm look that made her heart leap. Jess hung her coat on the coat rack near the bay window and dove in to help. The front door opened and Lindy appeared, fluttering around to kiss Chase and hug everyone else.

As Lindy went to the kitchen, Jess and Nina cleared the dusty jars of teas from behind the main counter, replacing them with a selection of wines. Lindy returned from the kitchen with her hands full of baked goods and began loading them into the newly fixed display case at the front, which was running nice and cool, thanks to a little tender loving care, courtesy of Mason. Wes zipped around, cleaning every inch of chrome and tile within his reach, even giving the jukebox a little buffing.

The old hardwood floors were swept and given a coat of polish that made them shine. New drapes went up. New chairs came in. Cal and Chase unloaded a delivery truck that pulled up, full of fresh produce and dry goods that weren't bought on credit with her vendors. Jess sent a silent thank you up for the immense success of the food truck, which was making all of this possible. Well, not just the food truck—she owed a lot of her progress to the man bringing the last of the new dining chairs in from the sidewalk.

Chase must have seen her staring because he stopped and returned the look that must have been on her own face—goofy, happy, lovestruck. She turned away and surveyed their progress, and then her eyes flicked to the clock on the wall. Had it been that long since they'd started? She always found that time zipped by when she was surrounded by the people she loved.

Nearby, Wesley and Nina replaced the old paper napkin dispensers with carefully folded linen napkins. Wes ran back and forth taking sets of new napkins to Nina as Lindy folded them. Jessica said, "Wes, Nina,

Lindy, way to go on the table decor."

Jess waved to Chase. "Ready to take a breather?"

Chase said, "Hey, this is my workout. I haven't hit the gym in weeks." He flexed. Jess rolled her eyes, and Nina giggled. Lindy swatted her son with a napkin.

Jessica said, "All right, gang, a few more hours to go. Into the kitchen!" Nina, Lindy, and Chase headed toward the kitchen. Wes ran up and hugged Jess before following the rest of the group in.

The next few hours passed in a flurry of food, chatter, and more than a few spills. Jess and Cal started on the featured stew while Nina carefully lined pie crusts with local peaches. Wes and Chase rolled dough at a third workstation, kept in line by some serious side-eye from Jess when a large round of dough ended up on Wes's head instead of on the kitchen counter. She couldn't help but laugh at the innocent expressions on both Chase and Wesley's faces as pie dough dripped into Wes's eyes.

When the last dish was slid into the oven, and the last pot was turned down to a simmer, Cal kicked everyone out of the kitchen. They regrouped at the front counter next to the stacks of new dishware for a snack. Jess and Chase bustled back and forth, bringing coffee for the adults and milk for Wesley, along with big plates of fresh brownies.

As the group relaxed, Chase came to embrace Jess, pride on his face.

"Is this what it feels like right before the big game?" she asked, leaning back as she clasped hands with him. She was amazed at how easy it had been for them to slip back into such cozy familiarity.

Chase said, "Yeah. Pretty much. By the way, I got you something. A little gift to celebrate tonight."

He handed her a box wrapped in ornate paper. She set

it on the counter and unwrapped it carefully. Inside, she found a frame that displayed a beautiful assortment of souvenir postcards from around the globe. She paused, struck by the beauty of the postcards, uncertain of what he was trying to say. Last time they'd talked about her dreams of travel, he'd been pointing out that she'd never followed them.

"If I remember correctly, you used to collect these," Chase said.

"These are all the places I was going to visit one day," she said, running her fingers over the touching gift.

Chase wrapped his hands around hers as she held the frame. "You went for your dream with the diner. Maybe it's not too late for all the other dreams?"

Jessica considered the thoughtfulness of the postcards and his help in the reopening. "Thank you, Chase," she said to him. She could never thank him enough.

A long moment passed as she studied him. They really did make a great team. And despite their past—her past—she was letting him in, and he seemed to be allowing her back into his heart. Each day that went by had her throwing caution to the wind more and more, feeling an increasing surety that he would somehow stay. She didn't want Chase to be here for one or two amazing weeks. She wanted him to be here for all of their ordinary days, and she wanted those days to pile up into all the weeks for the rest of their lives. The confession almost spilled out of her.

Chase's phone, sitting on the counter next to them, lit up. Chase ignored it.

"Are you going to get that?" Jess asked.

"I don't need any bad news. I want tonight to stay perfect," he said. He slid his thumb along the screen to reject the call and shoved the phone back into his pocket. "You looked like you were about to say something. Care to share?"

Cal called out from the kitchen. "Hey, Jess, I need your help in here for just a second."

As she strolled off to talk with Cal, she glanced back over her shoulder and said to Chase, "Yeah. I've got a killer dress for tonight, and I'm about to change into it. Don't go anywhere."

The look on his face was worth the little white lie.

Last-minute kitchen snafus were ironed out, Nina and Wes were all dressed up and standing at the ready, and Jessica had swapped her waitress uniform for the sleek, black dress she'd told Chase about. She had tried to convince Chase to at least come out front and grab a seat at the counter for the evening, but he'd insisted on staying in the kitchen and helping Cal in case the orders got too much for one cook to handle. Jess hoped they would be lucky enough to need Chase as a backup.

Chase was the only one in the back when she breezed into the kitchen, feeling nervous—and not just about the reopening.

Jessica said, "So, how do I look?" *And will you stay forever? Because I think I love you.*

Chase looked up and didn't speak for a long moment. Had she said what she was thinking aloud?

"Perfect," he said finally, his smile genuine. He held out his hands to her. She slid hers into his warm grasp. Should she tell him now? Would it ruin the evening?

She thought about how he'd ignored his phone call

in case it was bad news from his agent. Deciding that she didn't want to risk a reaction she wasn't prepared for in keeping with Chase's exact reasoning, she just kept smiling. Chase tugged her closer.

Nina poked her head in the kitchen. "Uh, guys?"

Jess blinked over at Nina, feeling her stomach lurch.

"I think it's time," Nina said.

Jess and Chase let out a breath together, and she squeezed his hands. Their eyes met one final time.

"Okay," she started, ready to give a pep talk that would mostly be for her benefit anyway.

"You got this," Chase said simply, which summed up everything she needed to hear.

They walked hand in hand out of the kitchen, and he released her as she scooted through the narrow pass and into the dining room. She wiped her sweaty palms on her dress and braved a look at the front door. Jess stopped short, and she heard the squeak of Nina's shoes behind her as both she and Chase also halted suddenly.

A large crowd of people waited outside to get in.

Nina, gleeful, said the words that Jess couldn't have forced out if she'd tried. "I'd say we got the word out."

Jess was in shock.

Chase said, "I'd say we did."

Jess felt pure joy well up from within her, and she couldn't fight the beaming smile that bloomed on her face. She fought back the tears, emotion evident in her voice as she gushed to Nina and Chase, "Thank you guys so much. For everything."

"Group hug!" Nina blurted, and Jess could hear that her friend was near tears herself.

"Yeah," Jess agreed, turning to fold both Nina and Chase into a big squeeze. She gestured to Cal and Wes, who stood at the front counter. Wes hopped off his stool and rushed over to add himself to the tangle. Cal just waved them off, throwing a clean towel over his shoulder as he went to unlock the door. Passing him on her way to the front, Jess saw her curmudgeonly cook wipe at his eyes as he headed back into the kitchen.

Jessica smiled as she watched him walk away. Taking a deep breath, she turned and threw open the diner's doors. People poured in.

As customers chattered excitedly and began to find their way to the tables, she greeted them. "Welcome to the new Wesley's!"

Wow, so many people. She looked back and saw Chase leaning beside Wes at the counter. Nina was already passing out menus. Jess was so glad that she wasn't alone in this. Her heart warmed, if possible, even more.

She started taking a quick survey of the restaurant, looking out over the tables and marking the number of guests that occupied each on her new floor map, which covered the top of the new podium near the front door. Among the guests pouring in was Charlie. Jess spotted him slipping in the door and made eye contact, which he tried to avoid.

Oh, no you don't, she thought.

"Charlie!" she called.

He reluctantly sauntered over to her.

"This is a surprise. Isn't your restaurant open tonight?" she asked.

He tucked his hands, adorned with several expensive rings, into the pockets of his expensive suit pants. He surveyed the diner noncommittally.

"Oh, of course. I just thought I would turn out to help support a fellow restaurateur," Charlie said. The sly grin that slid onto his face was as off-putting as his cologne. "And, you know, scope out the local competition."

Jessica grabbed a menu and laughed, trying not to breathe too deeply. "Hmmm. Well, I hope you enjoy. Let me show you to your table."

She led Charlie to a small two-top table with a view of the whole dining room. She avoided putting him where she'd wanted to—at the one rickety table she'd left in a corner near the bathrooms, a table which currently held extra napkins and silverware waiting to be rolled.

"How's this?" Jess asked, gesturing to the prime spot. Charlie nodded his approval, and she left his menu and breezed away to make a turn around the rest of the guests. Nina bustled back and forth, taking orders, and Jess picked up a water pitcher, ready to help out. As she was pouring water for a table near the counter, she glanced up to see Chase and Wesley looking proudly at the bustling dining room.

Chase said, "Well, I think we did it, kiddo."

Jess heard Wes respond. "We sure did."

The pride in her son's voice was equal to any she'd heard when he talked about acing a test, clearing a level in his space wars game, or finally getting a hit in baseball. She watched Chase and Wes exchange a fist bump. Chase headed back into the kitchen, and Jess beamed as she moved to the next table.

The kitchen was just starting to hop. Chase rolled up his sleeves and tied on an apron. He grabbed the first ticket from the few orders that were already clipped to the pass. Two stews to start. Chase picked up a ladle and sampled a spoonful of stew. He added some seasoning, looking over his shoulder at Cal.

"I got starters," Chase offered. "I'll mark 'em as I send 'em and pass entrée orders to you. Sound good?"

Cal nodded and came to scan the tickets that still hung next to Chase. "Looks like the ravioli is going to be popular," Cal said. "I'd better go pull some more from the deep freeze."

As Cal hustled out of the kitchen to the freezer, Chase's phone rang. This made the third time tonight he'd gotten a call from Spencer. Chase hadn't been lying to Jess when he'd told her that he was avoiding bad news. He didn't want to talk to his agent, didn't want to hear the note of pity in the man's voice as he told Chase, yet again, to keep his chin up and his hopes alive. The phone went silent but immediately rang again. After waffling for as long as he could, Chase put down the spoon and answered.

Chase said, "Hey, Spence."

Spencer's voice wasn't full of pity, as Chase had expected. Instead, he sounded jubilant. "Chase, why haven't you returned my calls? Never mind. I got news!" Spencer paused to up the suspense. Chase's heart rate jumped as the seconds ticked by.

"You're officially back!" Spencer announced and then fell silent, waiting for Chase's response.

But Chase, too, was silent. He couldn't respond. He should be asking for details—what city, what terms, what position, how much money? But the most important question was one that he couldn't even begin to ask— how soon would he have to leave?

"Chase, are you listening? You're back in business!"

Chase stammered. "Back? Back where? Boston?" Why wasn't he thrilled to hear that he'd landed a new deal? He could go back to his old life full of luxuries, parties, and adoring fans. *But no Jess. No Wesley.*

Spencer said, "Better than that! Southern California! And they want you there immediately."

"I…but…so soon?" Chase heaved out a heavy breath that did nothing to lift the weight that suddenly slammed down onto his shoulders.

"I know. Fantastic, right?" Chase heard Spencer thump his palm on his desk, the sound so loud that it was clear, even through the phone. "You are on your way. Start packing those bags, pal. You're back in the game!"

Chase's throat constricted. Pack his bags? Leave *immediately*?

"Chase? Hello? Chase, buddy, listen to me. Second chances like this don't come by every day."

Cal banged back into the kitchen, carrying a big metal tub of ravioli that had been portioned neatly into plastic bags.

Chase said, "I'm going to call you back, okay, Spence?" He didn't wait for his agent to reply. He disconnected the call and tried unsuccessfully to shake off the constricting feeling squeezing the air out of his lungs. He took a steadying breath. Cal eyed him.

"You okay?" the older man asked.

"Yeah, I'm fine, thanks." Chase put his phone back into his pocket.

Jessica swept in, and Chase looked up. The same feeling came back, and he knew now what it was—panic. If he left, where would that leave them?

"Chase, how's the stew coming?" Jess asked. Chase realized he hadn't even filled the soup orders that he'd promised to. He froze, his mouth open. Jessica frowned at him and then put a gentle hand on his arm.

"You okay? You look stressed," she said. "*I'm* the one who's supposed to be stressing out."

Her smile brought Chase back to reality. It was a smile he would have to leave behind, for the second time in a lifetime, if he accepted the offer Spencer was so excited about.

"Yeah. Yeah! This is just my game face," he assured her.

Jessica nodded slowly, but he knew she must be sensing that something was off. She poked him playfully with the pen in her hand, tearing a new order off her order pad and hanging it up with the others. "Well, come on, chop-chop, stir-stir. We have a full house out there. Let's keep up the pace!"

She spun dramatically and bustled back to the dining room.

"All right, boss." He threw a little good-natured attitude at her retreating form, turning to the stove. He waited until she was gone from the kitchen, the click of her heels fading from earshot, before he pulled his phone out and hit the button to power it completely off.

Chapter 17

*T*HE EVENING WAS WINDING DOWN, the packed restaurant filled with satisfied diners. Jess's new recipe for peach pie had been expertly executed by Nina earlier that day, and warm slices had been delivered to the diners who were now lingering over dessert. Browned-butter caramel sauce dripped from the cardamom-spiced ice cream that crowned the pie slices, and soon, the sounds in the dining room quieted to just the clink of dessert spoons hitting empty plates.

Jess was standing by the front door, erasing the marked tables from her diagram as each group of diners exited. She didn't see Charlie rise and head toward the door at first. When she did look up and spot him, he didn't avoid her this time, instead swaggering up to where she stood and clearing his throat.

She smiled thinly, bracing for more of his cutting banter. "So what'd you think?" she asked.

Charlie said neutrally, "It was okay." Something about his posture, though, was more relaxed, friendlier than when he'd come in. His shirt button was undone at the neck, and Jess had noticed that he'd even shrugged out of his jacket as he'd eaten, though the garment was now back on.

Jessica pushed for more, wondering if she would even gain anything from an elaboration. "Just okay?"

Charlie admitted magnanimously, "Well, actually, the risotto was superb." He patted his stomach, smiling.

Jessica relaxed a little. He'd come to the diner tonight likely expecting a terrible experience, and they'd made him a happy customer. "Wow, that means a lot coming from you."

Charlie leaned in and lowered his voice as if he didn't want to be overheard. "Well, it looks like the competition has just upped its game."

Jessica laughed and couldn't resist razzing him just a bit. "A little competition never hurt anyone. I have a feeling we're both gonna be just fine. Good night, Charlie."

Charlie smiled and rapped his knuckles on her podium. "Good night, Jessica. Don't change that risotto." She watched as he walked out, feeling a deep sense of accomplishment.

Jess stayed at the front to say good night to every customer who left afterward, basking in the congratulations and compliments of dozens of friendly faces. Cal headed out, followed by Nina, who carried a sleeping Wesley. Jess reminded Nina to set the alarm before she crashed in the guest room since they would have to be up early to reopen for breakfast—the plan was to be in an hour before their normal time to allow for any unforeseen hiccups with the new breakfast menu. Jess kissed Wes's forehead, and then she was alone in the diner.

Parker Falls had all but forgotten about her diner. It had been old news. But tonight, they'd come back.

Speaking of coming back...

Jess thought of Chase as she pulled down the shade on the front door and clicked the lock into place. Now that they could finally catch a moment alone, it was time she talked to him about her feelings. She flipped the light switches off through the dining room as she headed to the kitchen, following the lone sounds of activity that echoed from the back and through the empty restaurant.

She found him wiping flour off the butcher's block in the kitchen. He stood as she entered. Feeling giddy and triumphant, she launched herself at him as he turned.

"We did it," she said. "We did it!"

His arms enfolded her. He pulled her close, and the strength of him seeped into her. The embrace lasted, but not as long as Jess would have liked. Chase pulled away with the same look in his eyes as the night of the auction. Jess stayed pressed against him, waiting to relive that moment—that tenderness, that kiss. It would be the perfect foil for her confession. It would certainly give her the courage she needed to tell him that she'd fallen for him again.

The moment lost its charge as, abruptly, Chase stepped back. He squeezed her arms briefly and then broke their physical contact.

Chase looked away from her as he said, "I should, uh, probably go."

Jessica protested, pouting. "No! It's only nine o'clock. Celebrate with me. Kiwi tarts and ice cream and Spring Fling?" She grabbed both his hands, wrapping them around her waist again and stepping back into him. He groaned as if she were keeping him out when he was already past curfew, and his smile was thin. Something wasn't right. His mind seemed elsewhere. His posture hadn't relaxed, and he held her stiffly.

Chase sighed. "I wish I could. But, you know, you should be really proud of yourself. You took a big risk."

And I want to take a bigger one on you. Jess, her misgivings invading, kept the thought to herself.

"And I think it paid off," she said instead. "Thank you for everything."

"My pleasure."

There was a brief moment where she saw the urge to kiss her flicker again in his eyes. She tilted her head back, gazing up at him encouragingly. He tugged her toward him, closed the space between them, and brushed a kiss over her cheek.

Stepping away, he gave her hand one last squeeze before he slipped away and disappeared into the darkened dining room, leaving her standing in the kitchen with an unsettling feeling that her dream reunion just might be nearing its expiration date.

Chase had faced down impossible odds to have the career of his dreams, established himself as a sports star from his rookie season, pulled out winning games when it had seemed impossible by choosing just the right pitch. Baseball had made him famous, had made him wealthy—but had it made him *happy*? Chase leaned on a column at the corner of his parents' front porch, too conflicted to go in and face his folks. His mom would spot his angst right away, and Chase didn't want to trouble her.

The chilly night air didn't bother him nearly as much as the memory of the bewildered look that had been on Jess's face as he'd left the diner. He hadn't told her about the phone call from Spencer or about his offer because the reopening had been so perfect for her. He wouldn't have been able to stand being the reason her triumphant night was ruined. He knew that he had to tell her. He had to tell Wesley. Chase couldn't just take off—it smacked of the exact way he'd left all those years ago, and he wasn't an impulsive kid anymore.

Chase gazed up at the stars, shoving his hands into his pockets to warm them. His knuckles brushed his phone, which he still hadn't switched back on. He hadn't returned Spencer's call like he'd promised, either. Maybe Chase's indecision would end up making the decision for him. No, that was a cowardly way out. He needed to decide—fast.

The front door to his parents' house creaked softly, and Mason strolled out.

"What are you doing out here?" his dad asked, coming to stand beside Chase. "It's cold."

Chase said, "It's cold inside, too."

Mason nodded. "You know your mother. The furnace is off-limits after the first day of spring." He was silent for a moment. "So. How did things go tonight?"

"Perfect," Chase replied, knowing that the tone of his voice made the word antithetical.

"So why the long face?" Mason crossed his arms over his chest, and Chase studied his father. Chase wasn't used to asking his dad for advice, but this week had noticeably changed both of them. Mason was listening, waiting for Chase to speak. Chase decided that it was high time to let it all out.

Chase said, "I got an offer, Dad. In southern California."

Mason slapped Wesley on the back, his face lighting up. "That's fantastic! Right?"

"No, it's complicated," Chase admitted. He searched for the words to explain to his father, who'd been married to his mother for a lifetime and was light-years away from any angst when it came to romance.

Mason didn't need an explanation. He nodded in understanding. "Jessica?"

Chase nodded back.

Mason said, "I thought as much. How soon until ya gotta be there?"

"I have to leave right away." Chase had the sudden realization that it wasn't just his relationship with Jessica that would be on the line—whatever progress he and Mason had made might be strained again if Chase went back to his old life.

Mason, once again, seemed to know what Chase was thinking. "And if you go, we won't know if or when you'll be back. Right?"

Chase managed to nod again, a heavy feeling in his chest making words impossible.

"Hmm, I see. That is a pretty serious problem."

Chase was surprised that his dad didn't barrel in and bulldoze Chase with his own opinion on the situation. Mason stood, hands on hips, just listening. Chase swallowed and dropped his last bombshell.

"Yeah. And I promised Wesley that I'd play in the father-son baseball game with him."

Mason said, "So no matter what ya do, something's got to give."

"You know, Dad, I know I don't usually ask your

advice, but what should I do?" Chase, mostly from habit, braced for the trip down the one-way street of his father's worldview.

"That's a tough one," his dad started. "I've made a lot of mistakes in my life, even a few with your mother."

Chase said, "Really?"

"Did you know I almost didn't ask her to marry me? I bought the ring and all. Then I got an offer to work a pit crew in North Carolina."

Chase was aghast, his surprise at Mason's openness spurring him to ask, "Then what happened? How'd you make your decision?"

Mason said, "Well, simple, actually. I got out a piece of paper, and I wrote down everything I had to gain and everything I had to lose if I took the job."

"And what did you have on the list?"

Mason's expression was far away as he thought back. "One column was full—it was more money, opportunity, travel. The other column only had one word in it."

Chase knew before he asked, and he felt a slow smile lift his glum mood the barest fraction. "What was the word?"

Mason paused. "Lindy. I realized the only column that mattered was the one with her name on it." He smiled. "Most things in life that seem complicated are really pretty simple if you take a good, hard look."

Mason gave Chase a fatherly slug on the shoulder, leaving him on the porch beneath the stars, alone with his still-conflicted thoughts.

Chase had always thought of his father as an emotionless man, given more to the practical side of things, rather than someone who put stock in matters of the heart. Chase felt his sense of respect for his dad grow. Mason could change, and Chase *had* changed over this past week. But would turning down this offer be giving up his dreams—the very thing he'd told Jess not to do? Chase stared up at the twinkling stars, wishing the cold Ohio night would show him more than just the flyaway wisps of his own breath, curling out to disappear into the dark.

Chapter 18

*J*ESSICA WAS ON CLOUD NINE as she emptied the cash register to fill a bank deposit pouch. If her count was right—and she'd counted three times—this would not only bring the diner current with the bank but actually put them ahead a little. All of this from just a few busy meals and a couple of turns in the food truck. Finishing the task, Jess waved Nina over. Cal was off to lunch, so Jess could be a little silly with her friend without any withering looks or good-natured ribbing from the cook.

Jessica said, "Ready for the *most* important job in the world?"

Nina tossed down the towel she'd been using, bouncing toward Jess. "More important than cleaning the deep fryer?"

Jess made a face, thinking about cleaning the deep fryer. She zipped the pouch closed and handed it to Nina. "Run this down to the bank," Jess instructed, holding the pouch out as though the case itself were made of gold. "It has been a long time since we have been in the black. And something tells me we're back to stay."

That something was not just the newly increased business

at the diner. Since the appearance of the WOW at the Spring Fling, Jess had landed two company picnic catering jobs and a birthday party that was 1950s-themed. She was already formulating a menu in her head for the birthday party.

Nina took the pouch reverently, her face serious. "I'll guard it with my life."

She headed out, and Jess watched her and laughed as Nina made mock-ninja moves on her way to the front door. Nina slid past Chase, who Jess hadn't been expecting to come in this morning. Jess smiled, a little wary about his appearance as she thought back to his odd goodbye from last night. She busied herself with sorting the remaining change into the appropriate spots in the register drawer.

"Hey, Jess," Chase greeted her.

"Hey," she said back. There was still something about his expression that didn't set her at ease.

"I need to tell you something," he blurted.

Her stomach dropped. She looked up from the register. "Okay," she said slowly.

"It's kind of important. Is—is Wes here?" His eyes swept around the diner nervously.

Jessica said, "I dropped him at school. He's so excited about the father-son game that he left his lunch in the car." She laughed, feeling like she had to force it out. She clung to the laugh, a life raft in the sea of her jangling nerves. "He's so proud that you are his partner. He wanted to get to school early to remind all of his friends. So, what's going on?"

Chase exhaled deeply. As she waited for him to speak, time seemed to stretch.

His words finally burst out of him. "Well, I've got an offer coming in, and they want to fly me to California to talk about my future." He followed the revelation with a shaky smile.

Her first reaction was a deep and sudden sadness that stole her breath. *He's going to leave. It's real.*

The look on her face must have been one of devastation because Chase frowned and started to move toward her. She recovered and smiled widely as she took off her apron and came around the counter to meet him instead.

"That's amazing!" Jessica said. "Congratulations!" Reaching him, she pulled him into a hug.

He hugged her back, the tenseness she'd noticed in his shoulders easing somewhat. She hoped that he couldn't feel her own stiff posture.

"There's one more thing," he continued. "Uh, they want me there now."

Jessica said, "Now? Well, how soon is now?"

Chase said, "Tomorrow. They want me there to-morrow."

"Wait, *tomorrow* tomorrow?" No. It couldn't be. There was no way the universe was that cruel. She could take the pain of losing Chase again. She had been there and done that. But Wes didn't deserve to be hurt again.

"Yeah," Chase said quietly. There was no mistaking that he knew what leaving immediately meant, both for Jess and for Wesley. Chase took her hands. She unconsciously pulled them back. She tried to maintain a brave front, but the burn in the back of her throat was increasing, and she could feel her lower lip start to tremble. "Wow. That is sudden."

Chase said, "I'm in shock, too."

"And Wesley's game tomorrow?" Jessica blurted.

Chase reached for her, hesitated, and then grasped her shoulders, rubbing his hands up and down her arms. She wanted to pull away. No, she wanted him to pull her in, tell her that he had changed his mind, or at least that he could eke out one more day with them. But the short distance that separated them remained, and she felt the first of her tears fall as he offered sadly, "I'm so, so sorry."

She'd lost him before, when she'd been a reckless and impulsive young woman, but there had been no one to suffer from the fallout but herself. Now she had Wes. Despite the tearing feeling that accompanied the knowledge that she was losing Chase again, despite the additional pain of knowing that she could have—should have—kept herself from getting attached so quickly, she had to keep it together. She'd known Chase would leave.

Jessica shook her head, swiping at the single tear and managing to hold back the rest that threatened. "No, hey, it's okay. It's okay. These things happen. And I am so happy for you, Chase. And Wesley is going to be really happy for you, too."

Chase's hands were still on her shoulders, and she knew that the gesture was an attempt to comfort himself as much as it was to comfort her. His own eyes were shining as he said, "I just…I didn't want it to go like this, you know?"

"I know," she assured him. Just like her tendency to hover and fret over Wes, she couldn't help but want to protect Chase. She didn't want Chase to hurt over having to leave them, even if it meant holding back her own misery for the moment. She knew that her desperate resolve not to cry would absolutely crumble later when she had a chance to fall apart where no one could see, but for now, it held.

"You deserve a second chance. And you got one," Jess reassured him. She paused a moment. "And thank you for reminding me I can dream big, too."

Chase swallowed. If there was anything left for him to say, Jess was afraid to hear it. If his next words were even close to the ones she'd wanted to say last night, she would find his leaving unbearable.

"Look—" he started.

Jessica cut him off quietly, pulling away. "Yeah, I gotta go. I need to get Wesley his lunch."

Chase said, "Well, maybe I'll come with you. I'd love to explain to Wes."

Jessica couldn't bear another minute of goodbye. She waved a hand in the air, brushing off his offer. That resolve not to cry? It was buckling under some serious pressure. She backpedaled toward the kitchen, feeling her tears threaten again. "Yeah, I think it's— I just need to handle it myself."

Chase said, "But—"

"Trust me. I've been there before." At Chase's hurt look, she tried to soften the unintentional slight. "Congratulations."

She hurried to the kitchen, stifling the first sob with the back of her hand. She heard him close the front door, and when enough time had passed that she was certain he wouldn't still be out there, she went to the dining room and flipped the sign on the door to Closed.

Chapter 19

*W*ITH BAD NEWS, YOU BREAK *it sooner rather than later, right?* Jessica knew she had to tell Wesley about Chase as soon as she could. The boy had talked about practically nothing else but the Parker Falls Father-Son Baseball Game for days. It meant so much to him, and now he was going to be crushed to learn that Chase wouldn't be there. Jessica wanted to be sure that she was the one who told him—soon, before he learned it from someone else.

After she'd allowed herself a good ten minutes to break down, Jess had flipped the diner sign back to open. She'd had to dodge Nina's questions when her friend had returned after the bank errand to find Jess a puffy-faced, crying mess. Jessica left the diner in the capable hands of Nina and Cal and went to meet Wes.

She wondered how she'd break the news to her son. She wondered how he'd react. Wesley had suffered so many disappointments in the last few years. He'd had so many losses for a kid his age. Jessica couldn't believe she had to explain to him about another. How could she tell her son that the one thing he'd been counting on had again been taken away by fate? What words would she use?

Jess made it home with time enough to wash her face and meet Wesley at the bus stop when he came home from school. She still hadn't decided how she would explain things when she parked the car in the driveway and walked the short distance down to the corner where Wesley's bus always let kids out.

She watched for the bus, absently swaying back and forth, frowning, thinking, and considering several different approaches as she waited. She saw the bus in the distance, and she tried to force her lips, which were pressed together tightly, into something resembling a smile.

The bus stopped right in front of her, and Wesley was the first one off, a giant smile on his own face. "Mom!" he exclaimed. She didn't normally meet him, and his exuberance was contagious.

His innocent happiness turned her own forced expression into something more natural, and Jessica grinned up at him. "Wes!"

"What are you doing here?"

"Oh, you know, I thought I'd come walk you home, spend a little time with you this afternoon," she said. He fell eagerly into step beside her.

The school bus pulled away from the bus stop as Jessica walked Wesley down the side of the road toward their house. The spring air still had a bit of a nip, and she and Wesley both wore light jackets. The sky was overcast, and it seemed to be promising rain. It fit with the way Jess was feeling inside—overcast, possibly stormy. As they walked, Wesley talked a mile a minute, tossing a baseball up and catching it as it dropped into his hands.

Wesley said, "So I told Tommy that Chase is gonna

play in the father-son game, and he's so jealous. It's awesome."

Wesley side-eyed her, trying to gauge her reaction, and Jessica manufactured a gentle laugh that ended with a smile. But she knew she couldn't stall on telling Wesley that Chase was leaving. She hated to do it, but she couldn't wait any longer.

Wesley went back to tossing his ball up and catching it as they continued to walk.

"Yeah, buddy," Jessica said, "about that…" She stared into the distance, searching for words. "There's been a bit of a complication."

Wesley looked up at her. "What d'ya mean?"

Please take this okay. She didn't want to see the hurt that she was afraid would be in her son's eyes. Two years ago, the pain in Wesley's eyes when Davis had left had been enough to last Jess a lifetime.

Jessica said, "Well, it looks like Chase is going to California and that they're gonna make him an offer."

Wesley's eyes lit up, and Jessica could tell that he just couldn't contain his excitement. He didn't know yet that what he was celebrating was going to mean disappointment for him.

"Yes!" he exclaimed.

Jessica laughed. Wes was so kind, with such a big heart. He was happy for Chase, even though he had to realize that the offer would take Chase away from Parker Falls.

"That is so cool," Wesley continued.

"I know," Jessica agreed.

"I told him to just be patient." Wesley seemed so sure of himself, as if he'd known the entire time, as if the universe was a place that made sense if you just had faith. Jessica hated the news she now had to deliver, the news that would take some of that confidence away from her son.

She threw her arm over Wesley's shoulder and drew him to her side.

"Aww. Yeah, well, that is the really cool part. But…" *Just do it. Give him some credit. He's a strong kid. And he's got you.*

Wesley began to throw the ball again as Jessica continued to talk.

"The uncool part is that it looks like he's got to be there tomorrow."

Wesley caught the ball and slowed to a stop as he began to realize what this meant.

"The same night as your game," Jess clarified softly.

Wesley frowned, his happy demeanor crumbling. He looked up at her. There it was, the pain that stabbed at her heart.

Wesley said, "So he won't be at our game?"

Jessica wished that she could take the pain away as quickly as she had caused it.

"No," she said, unable to find any more words to comfort him, feeling sadness descend on her, as well. Wesley's eyes dropped back down to the road. Jessica rallied and tried to put a better spin on the situation for him, something to look forward to, hoping to ease the disappointment that she could feel in Wesley's slumped shoulders.

"But you know what? He said he'd come back at the end of the season and maybe we could go up to Cleveland and watch him play this summer. Wouldn't that be fun?"

Wesley said, "I don't want to." His voice trembled.

Jessica, her heart in a million pieces, said, "Oh, Wesley."

Wesley raised his voice, frustrated. "Everybody makes promises 'cause it's easy. But it's also easy to break them."

"I know," Jessica said. "I know this really stinks."

"Everyone at school's gonna laugh at me," Wesley lamented.

"No, they won't," Jessica insisted. "Not if they're your real friends."

"I thought Chase was my real friend," Wes said plaintively.

"Hey, hey, hey." Jessica stopped and pulled Wesley to face her. She crouched in front of him and said, "He is your real friend. But sometimes even friends have to do things they don't want to."

Wesley shook his head sadly, turned, and ran up the sidewalk to their front door. Jessica watched him go, letting out a long, tense breath.

She knew it was going to be a tough night.

Once inside their home, Wesley changed from his school clothes without a word as Jessica tried to freshen herself up a little more after her hectic day. When she finished, she found Wesley leaning with his back against the kitchen counter, waiting for her. His eyes were downcast, his backpack sitting on the floor at his feet. As she entered the room, he grabbed the backpack full of books and headed out the front door without a word. Jessica scrambled to gather anything else they might need until the diner closed, knowing a busy dinner shift was ahead. She made sure the back door was locked and followed behind Wesley as he went straight to her car and climbed in the passenger seat.

They drove to the restaurant in silence, Wesley looking

down at the apparently very interesting shoes on his feet the entire way. Jessica parked behind the diner in her usual spot. The food truck sat behind the diner now, too, reminding Jess of everything that had transpired in the past two weeks. It was a bittersweet reminder.

Wesley was out of the car as soon as she put the vehicle in park, grabbing his backpack and heading for the door. Jessica followed, shaking her head sadly. She wanted to call him back, insist that he share what he was feeling with her, but another thing she'd learned recently stopped her. Chase had been right. Jess couldn't protect Wesley from everything, and she shouldn't smother him under the guise of concern. If he needed her, she knew that Wes would never doubt that she was always here.

By the time she made it inside, Wesley was already sitting down at his usual table in the corner, pushing aside the fancy new napkins and pulling books from his backpack. He spread them out in front of him. Jessica thought she'd give him a good amount of time to deal with the bad news on his own before she tried to make conversation with him.

When she thought back, she could see that Wesley often handled his emotions better if he was allowed to work things out on his own first without being pushed by anyone else. Still, all she wanted to do was give her son a hug and tell him that everything would be okay, that they'd work things out together.

Instead, she took a look around the restaurant. The place was almost empty. Only a couple of tables had customers. Although she could tell that Nina and Cal had been busy cleaning up from their incredible lunch rush, there was still a lot to do before the dinner rush began, and Jessica knew she'd need every minute to catch up. And maybe losing herself in diner chores would take her mind off Wesley's disappointment. And her own.

Jessica pitched in and helped as her crew cleaned menus, wiped tables and chairs, and swept the main floor in the restaurant. In the kitchen, they wiped counters, washed and stacked dishes and silverware, prepped food, and restocked the line for the evening's service. There was so much to do, and there remained a brief window before Parker Falls would begin to make dinner plans. Hopefully, her newfound popularity would hold for another meal.

The busyness was good. She'd been right. It had taken her mind off Chase. She'd only thought about his handsome face and how much she'd miss him once every minute or so during the entire time. A new record.

Before Jessica and her staff knew it, diners started to trickle through the door. The trickle became a stream. The stream became a torrent. And once again, the place was packed, with a line of diners waiting for open tables.

Everyone worked quickly, smiles on their faces, greeting diners, seating them, taking orders, and rushing them back to the kitchen. The kitchen rang with the sounds of Nina and Jess scurrying around to meet the demands of their hungry patrons and Cal hurrying to fill plates that slid onto the pass. Jessica loaded up a table's worth of plates on a tray and passed Nina on her way to deliver the food to the table.

Shoot, Jess thought. I *forgot to put up the order for table ten.*

Jessica inclined her head toward table ten and said, "Nina, that table needs two more duck ravioli and three of Grandpa's famous burgers with aioli fries. Can you write up the ticket for me?"

Nina said, "You got it."

Jess dropped off her tray full of food. Nina took several

orders, delivered the tickets to the kitchen, and headed back to the dining room. Just then, Jessica looked out and saw Brett walk in.

Jessica said, "Brett?" Apprehension flooded her. After the emotional wringer she'd been through today, she certainly didn't want an argument with Brett, and one in a restaurant packed with patrons seemed doubly unappealing.

He walked over to her with a cautious smile on his face. "Hi, Jess. I just wanted to stop in and say congrats." He took stock of the bustling restaurant. "Ignoring all my advice seems to have been the right call."

Jessica blew out her cheeks, relieved that Brett seemed to be extending an olive branch. "Thank you. I know you were just trying to help." She crossed her arms.

Brett said, "Sure. And Jess"—he raked his fingers through his hair nervously before continuing—"I'm sorry that I didn't treat you the best. I wasn't being fair to you by flaking out all those times, avoiding you. I should have been honest about my own feelings. I don't think we were meant for each other, but that's okay, too. You're amazing, and Chase is a lucky guy."

She couldn't admit to Brett that Chase was gone. She didn't want to wallow in pity—self-pity or sympathy from anyone else.

Jessica unfolded her arms to extend her hands to Brett. He took them, and they both smiled at one another. "I appreciate your honesty. Somewhere out there is the perfect girl for you. And you are welcome here, among friends, whenever you'd like."

Nina zipped by, shooting a questioning look at Jess. Suddenly, Jess thought of something.

"You know, I may have a lead on some new business for you," she said to Brett.

He looked at her with curiosity, glancing around the restaurant again.

Jess called to Nina. "To go order, Nina!"

Nina came over so quickly that Jess knew she'd been waiting for a cue. What her friend didn't know was that this time, Jess had a little matchmaking scheme cooking for *her*.

"Yeah, boss?" Nina asked, taking out her order pad.

Jessica asked, "Nina. How many fender benders did you get in last month?"

Nina considered the question. Reluctantly, she counted on her fingers, finally admitting, "Five-ish?"

"Brett, Nina's due for a break soon. Let's get you some dinner on the house, and while you wait, let me send desserts over to that empty booth. Maybe you can tell Nina about your best coverage plan," Jess suggested.

Brett looked at Jess, looked at Nina, and then said, "Um…sure."

Jess handed Brett a menu, pointed him toward the only empty booth in the diner, and smiled as she moved behind the counter to slice two orders of pie.

Nina, after studying Jess's face for signs of stress, said, "Thanks, boss. And table five's feeling a little down about a baseball game. Think some of our world's best spaghetti and meatballs might help?"

Jess nodded, handing over the pie plates to Nina. Nina grinned ridiculously and went to sit down with Brett, casting a look at Jess that seemed to say, *"Are you kidding me?"* Jess gave her friend a warm look in return. Nina's grin didn't waver as she slid into the booth opposite Brett. The woman was practically bouncing in her seat.

Jessica checked on Wes, who was huddled over his books, still glowering just a bit.

"World's best spaghetti, coming up," she said to

herself. She headed to the kitchen and handed Cal the order for her son. While Cal prepared Wesley's favorite pasta, Jessica took a few moments to wipe down the kitchen line from the dinner rush.

As she finished clearing old order tickets from the check spindle at the end of the pass-through, Cal called, "Order up, Jess!"

Jessica grabbed the warm plate of steaming pasta and carried it across the diner to a corner where Wes was doing his homework. Jessica watched him concentrating on his books as she approached. He seemed less sullen than he had just a short time ago. She knew the hurt wasn't gone—not by a long shot—but maybe he'd accepted the reality of the disappointment.

Jessica delivered the spaghetti to her son. She'd made sure to write down an extra piece of cheese bread, too. "I know that homework's important, but how about a break?"

Wesley said, "Thanks, Mom. So...think Chase is gone yet?"

Jessica didn't know. She'd been too upset to ask anything about his schedule when Chase had told her he was leaving. When was his flight? Maybe he was already on his way to the airport. Maybe he was already most of the way to California. Maybe he wasn't even leaving until tomorrow. She could try to call and check, but it would just rip off the bandage when the bullet hole was still fresh.

"I'm not sure," she said. "But just know that I'm not going anywhere. Okay?"

Wesley said, "Okay." He picked up one of the gooey pieces of bread and dipped it into his spaghetti. He took a big bite.

"And hey," Jess added. "I was thinking. If business

keeps going like this, maybe we can take a vacation this summer. Visit a couple of those places we've been reading about?"

Wesley stabbed a meatball and, with his mouth full, said, "You bet, Mom."

He smiled up at Jess, sauce on his face, and it was just the ray of sunshine she needed to push her own wavering mood back to the bright side.

Chapter 20

A SPRING RAINSTORM HAD FALLEN ON Parker Falls while they slept. Though the raindrops had finally stopped, the early morning remained overcast and gray, and dim sunlight shone through rain-streaked kitchen windows in the Taynor house.

Chase sat at the table with Mason and Lindy, their breakfasts sitting untouched in front of them. Nobody seemed to have much appetite this morning. They'd been talking about the surprise offer that Chase had received, and there was a tension in the air. Chase thought his parents would have been more excited about his prospects for returning to the league. Heck, Chase thought he'd have been more excited. But something about leaving Parker Falls didn't sit right with him. Something felt unfinished, incomplete. Maybe it was the weather that had him feeling a bit gloomy.

Chase said, "You know, I'm actually surprised. I thought I was all washed-up."

Mason and Lindy both laughed softly. Or were they just releasing the breaths they'd been holding? Chase wished that someone would just say what they were thinking instead of keeping up the polite façade that everything was hunky-dory. That had caused their family all kinds of strain.

Lindy said, "Well, I'm proud of you, son. It's just…" She trailed off, looking down at her untouched plate of food.

Chase could tell something was bothering her about his news. Feeling suddenly annoyed, he pushed away his own misgivings about leaving. Why wasn't anyone happier about his chance to return to the one thing in his life that had always made sense, the one thing he'd always dreamed of doing? Sure, he'd had a great few weeks here, but he'd busted his tail in the league, and they were welcoming him back, even after everything that had happened. Who got that kind of a second chance?

"Just what?" Chase asked when she didn't finish her sentence.

Lindy smiled at him. Her eyes cut to Mason as she said, "We see how happy you already are—here."

Chase had to admit that his mother was right. She was always right. "Yeah," he said, "it's true, Mom. I know." Chase felt as though he had to explain. He had to make them understand why he was choosing to leave. He turned his attention to Mason. "But this is my shot."

Mason said, "We get it, son. It's just Jessica is one in a million."

Well, at least his dad got right to it. Clearly, his parents had spoken to each other about this because Lindy picked it up from there. "And we're a little afraid that if you go, you won't come back."

Chase didn't reply for a moment. The thought of never coming back scared him as much as the thought of turning down the offer and ending his career.

Finally, he said, "I'll be back. I promise."

Lindy looked across the table at Mason, a sadness in her eyes. She let her gaze drop down to the table again.

Mason sighed and grasped his wife's hand. Chase could tell they'd said what they wanted to say. Even if they thought he hadn't, Chase *had* thought about this. He'd made up his mind. He knew what he was leaving behind, but he also knew that baseball was all he'd ever wanted in life. Nothing meant more to him. Did it?

Mason rose, saying, "Well, we better get a move on it then." He patted Chase on the shoulder and headed out of the kitchen to load Chase's luggage into the car.

Lindy's eyes welled with tears. Chase pushed away from the table, giving his mother a smile.

"Come here, Mom," he said. He opened his arms to her.

"I'll miss you," Lindy said as she stood to hug her son.

Chase towered over his mother, but he knew that in her eyes, he'd always be her little boy. And now he knew the feeling—Chase had grown to care for Wesley the same way.

"It's okay," Chase said to Lindy. "I'll be back." Chase was also all-too-aware that he'd promised the same before.

Chase helped his dad load his luggage in the car. It didn't take them long—the Mercedes didn't have much space for luggage anyway—and before Chase knew it, the time had come for him to leave. Chase hated goodbyes. He supposed he'd gotten that from his mom, who cried again as she hugged him. Mason, too, wrapped his arms around Chase.

Chase told them both he loved them, and he promised again that he'd be back soon. Then he climbed into his car and pulled onto the wet streets of Parker Falls, headed for the airport. He couldn't believe he was leaving again—and so soon. His visit now seemed so brief. Chase knew he'd miss the town he'd grown up in; he always did. But he also knew that another chance at a career in baseball awaited him at the other end of his flight.

A nagging feeling continued to bother him as he drove. He'd left Parker Falls before, but something was different this time. And he knew what it was: Jessica and Wesley.

Parker Falls was his home. It was where he'd been born, where he'd grown up, where he'd gone to school, learned to ride a bike and throw a baseball. He remembered the streets and houses and businesses and people he'd known as a youth. They'd all helped to make him. They'd shaped him into the man he was today. Many of them had even tried to comfort him since he'd returned, and he'd brushed them off, too uncomfortable reliving his failure to recognize that what the town offered him was love, acceptance.

Yes, Parker Falls had shaped him. But Jessica and Wesley had done more than that. They'd become a part of his life. They'd become a part of *him*. And it felt to Chase as if he was leaving a part of himself behind, a part he might never get back.

Parker Falls would always be there, and Chase could always return to find his hometown almost unchanged. The same couldn't be said for Jessica and Wesley. Would *they* always be there? Would they wait for him? Time changed people, for better and for worse. They would continue to live, to laugh, to grow, and to love whether Chase was there or not. There was the chance that Jess and Wesley would move on without him.

The thought of Wesley's disappointment, and the fact that Chase had left without explaining to the boy in person, weighed heavily on Chase. There would be other baseball games, but there would never be *this* game, the one where Chase had let Wesley down. As he drove, Chase reflected on how, just a few days ago, all he'd been worried about was his own disappointment and possibly failing career.

But now Chase's future called. Baseball called. Another chance at the big show. Who, in the real world, ever got two chances at the dream of a lifetime? *Two* chances. Only this time, it felt as though he'd have to lose a piece of himself that he'd just rediscovered for that second chance. How could he decide to do that, to leave a part of himself behind in order to grab hold of a dream?

Chase gripped his steering wheel tighter. Why did things have to be so complicated?

He sighed, easing up on the gas pedal. There was still time before his flight. He could slow down a little and think.

Did things *have* to be so complicated? What was it that his dad had told him—that things were actually simple? A list with two columns. That's what Mason had done, right? Chase could do that, too. Of course, he couldn't safely do that while driving.

Chase saw the park coming up ahead. He could pull over there. The parking lot would work as well as any place. Chase checked his rearview and side mirrors for traffic. Signaling a left turn and checking his mirrors again, he pulled the Mercedes into the lot that overlooked the beautiful park. Trying not to think about the last time he'd been out here with Jessica, Chase eased into a spot, put the car in park, and turned the key in the ignition to kill the engine. The silence that descended robbed him of all distractions.

He took a deep breath as he stared out through the windshield. Chase thought the brisk, damp, spring air would help him think, so he climbed out of his car and went to the passenger side. He opened the passenger door and reached into the glovebox, where he found the car rental agreement. He pulled it out, taking it as a sign that the pen he'd used on the agreement was still clipped to the bundle of papers. He shut the car door and began to walk, pulling the pen free from the papers and clicking it. Chase paused at the entrance to the park and looked out across the expanse.

Walkers and joggers were making their way around the park's paths, some of them circling the pond at the park's center. A boy and his father were tossing a baseball back and forth, and Chase now tied the memory of doing the same thing with his own dad when he'd been that age with coaching Wes.

That was where it had started, Chase guessed, just having a toss with Mason. And the skills he'd learned had taken him to the top. It had been his own reckless behavior and hard living that had sent him crashing to the bottom. Jess and Wesley hadn't cared who he'd been before he came back to Parker Falls. Jess had known who he was before he'd left it, and that had seemed good enough for her.

Chase gazed down at the nearly empty back of the rental agreement. Holding the paper in his left hand and the pen in his other, he began to write. He made two columns: *SoCal* and *Parker Falls*. He drew a line between them, the line separating his past and his future. But which was which?

Chase started to jot things down in the two columns as they occurred to him. Under *SoCal*, he wrote, *Career*. And in that same column, he wrote, *Salary* and *Condo* and *Beaches* and *New Experiences* and *Connections*. This was what California held for him. He considered these things, looking out over the park. There was a lot in the first column.

Some townspeople walked past Chase, smiling as they recognized him. Chase smiled back, but he quickly averted his eyes, hoping to avoid a conversation. He needed time to think. He looked down at his two columns again. The *Parker Falls* column was empty.

Chase moved his pen to the empty space under *Parker Falls*. He wrote the name *Jessica*. As he studied her name for a moment, he thought about their pasts. His mind went over the last two weeks they'd spent together. He knew he'd grown closer to her in this short time than in all the time they'd spent together as kids. She meant so much more to him now than she had then.

Chase looked back up at the father and son throwing the ball. He wondered if either of them realized how important what they were doing was, that time shared together, the connection. Chase scrutinized the paper in his hands. Then he wrote *Wesley*. He eyed the two contrasting sides of the ledger as he thought about the past *and* the future.

Two columns. But which was the past and which was the future?

Chase studied the paper again and made up his mind. He went back to his car, climbed into the driver's seat, and started the engine. Hitting the button on the steering wheel that allowed him to make a hands-free call, he dialed Spencer's number.

When his agent picked up, Chase couldn't keep the excitement out of his voice.

"Spencer, my man," Chase greeted him. "I have great news."

Chase pulled out of the parking lot and began to drive. The future waited.

Chapter 21

"**L**ADIES AND GENTLEMEN, WELCOME TO the for-ty-second annual Parker Falls Father-Son Baseball Game!" The game announcer's voice boomed over the field from his vantage point in the press box. The press box had the advantage of being atop the concession stand behind home plate, so there was the added benefit of elevation to send the announcer's voice rolling out loudly over the assembled onlookers.

Clear blue skies domed the baseball field. Despite the spring date, the air was crisp and a bit cold, and the stands were filled with enthusiastic townsfolk wearing light jackets, including the mayor, Mason, Lindy, Cal, Nina, and Brett. They watched as the umpire dusted off home plate and stepped back.

Red and blue, the two teams stood down the opposing sides of the field along the baselines that extended out from home plate, each kid with a parent by his side. Wesley and Jessica were next to each other at the end of the blue line, just in front of their dugout. Jess tried not to squirm as, two by two, the announcer began to call out the names of the players on the field and their fathers, introducing them to the fans, who cheered politely as the roll was called.

"Playing on the blue team, Scott and Mike Smith," the announcer called.

The father and son smiled as the audience clapped.

The announcer continued. "Steve and Finch Monroe."

More applause.

"Gordon and Ronnie Runyon."

Jess winced and counted the number of father-son duos still left to call out.

"Jeff and Cole Campbell."

There were cheers as the Campbells, eight and thirty-five, tipped their caps. Jess knew Cole, a local farmer, from the many times she'd purchased produce from his farm. Only one more duo to go.

"Ben and Brian Callahan," the announcer bellowed.

The Callahans, nine and forty, waved to the crowd. Jess winced at what was coming next. She gripped Wes tightly, an arm around his shoulders. The gesture was to keep her upright.

The announcer called, "And Jessica and Wesley Parker."

Wesley's eyes were glued to the ground. Jessica squeezed the boy's shoulders again, this time for his benefit.

"You okay, Wes?" she asked.

Wesley looked up at his mom. The disappointment on his face was obvious to Jessica. But Wesley nodded, his lips pressed tightly together, and then went right back to staring at the ground.

"I know you wanted Chase to be here," Jessica said. What she didn't say was, *I want Chase to be here, too.* Chase had made his decision. She would have to live with it, no matter how much it tore at her heart. Chase had gotten his second chance, and it had just worked out that it had to happen at the expense of his and Jessica's second chance. She had been foolish to hope. Who, in the real world, ever got two chances at the dream of a lifetime? *Two* chances.

Wesley looked up at his mother again. "I'm just glad you're here, Mom."

Jessica smiled. She was touched by the brave face Wesley was putting on, suspecting strongly that he was doing it for her. She pulled him closer and hugged him tightly.

"Hold on," the announcer called unexpectedly, a rise in his voice. "There's one more player."

Jessica and Wesley both turned around in surprise, looking toward the announcer's booth. They weren't alone—every head in the stands swiveled. Dozens of hands came up to shield the sun from squinting eyes. Jessica held her breath.

It couldn't be.

She saw Chase make his way around the corner of the building. The crowd in the stands recognized their hometown hero and began to applaud. Chase jogged through an opening in the fence, smiling and waving to the crowd as he headed onto the field.

Jessica's gaze widened as her heart leaped. She fought to control the tears that threatened to fill her eyes, and her breath released in a near laugh of joy that she managed to corral into a smile as Chase trotted toward them.

Jessica watched as the fans continued to cheer wildly. In the stands, she saw Mason and Lindy exchange a knowing look, and Mason threw his fingers to his mouth and whistled loudly for his son. The two parents beamed, and Jessica didn't think she'd ever seen them looking so proud of their son. Had they known Chase was coming back? She'd thought it a little unusual that they had shown up at the game but had written the gesture off as one of sympathy.

Jessica marveled at Chase as he neared, struck by how handsome he was as he smiled graciously and humbly at the applause. He slowed his pace when he hit home plate and walked down the line of players.

Jessica looked back at the stands where Brett, Nina, and Cal sat together, laughing and cheering for Chase. She did a slight double take. Was Nina sitting a little closer to Brett than casual friends might? Jess's eyes turned back to Chase once more as he walked up to Wesley and her.

"Hey," Chase said, his greeting subdued. Wordless, almost unable to believe that he was here, Jess and Wesley shifted to the side, and Chase moved into place beside them. Wesley stared up at Chase with joy in his eyes.

Jessica pressed her lips together and tried to suppress the smile on her face. She attempted to hide beneath the bill of her baseball cap as she said casually, "You're a little late."

Chase said, "Well, I'm sorry. But"—he reached up and pulled the cap from her head and looked straight into her eyes—"I had a bit of a busy day."

She managed to stop smiling for a moment as she met Chase's gaze. "What'd you come back for?" she asked, her expression now more serious. There was a chance that he'd returned only for the game, so she didn't let her racing heart take over her practical head. At least, not for now.

Chase smiled at her. "Two reasons," he said. He regarded each of them in turn, Jess first, and then Wesley. "You. And you."

Unable to contain himself, Wesley dove for Chase and wrapped his arms around the man. Jessica laughed as her heart filled.

Jessica asked, needing to hear him say that he was staying, "And what happens *after* the game?" She paused. "Off to the airport for the red-eye to the coast?"

Wesley let go of Chase and stepped back in line beside his mother. Jessica placed an arm around her son's shoulder as she listened to Chase explain. Wes tensed beside her, waiting for the same confirmation.

Chase said, "I accepted a new offer." He paused dramatically. "Just one where I'm not a pitcher."

Jessica was puzzled. "I don't understand."

"Well, it turns out they wanted to hire me as a pitching coach," Chase explained. "So I called and made them a counteroffer." He paused again as she searched his eyes. "To be a scout for the Midwest. Based in Parker Falls."

Jessica laughed again, her face glowing. "Are you *serious?*"

She glanced at Wesley, who was beginning to understand that Chase was back for good—for them.

Chase grinned. "Well, yeah. You know I've got an eye for talent." He looked pointedly at Wes before he continued. "And besides, the traffic's a lot better here than out there. And I can set my own schedule, so…"

Still smiling, hardly believing this was real, Jessica prompted him, "So?"

"So I figured since Wesley's coach is retiring," Chase said, "I can maybe step in."

"That's awesome!" Wesley exclaimed.

He'd said it. He'd said that he was staying. Jessica couldn't suppress another laugh. Chase stared into her eyes and tilted his head to the side toward the baseball field. Jessica slid her arm from Wesley's shoulder and grabbed Chase's arm with both hands as he led her out of the line toward the center of the field. What more could he have to say? Her head was spinning with the day's revelations already.

"Not a lot of privacy in this town," Jessica said as they left their team's players and Wesley near home plate, walking to the pitcher's mound. The players, the fans, everyone was watching. Jessica knew that every townsperson here was very aware that something big was happening with Chase and her. The entire stands were silent, and all the spectators leaned forward, craning to hear as Jess and Chase moved farther away. Jess was surprised the announcer wasn't calling the play-by-play.

The crowd began to cheer and whoop as Jessica and Chase moved closer together. She gazed up at him, recognizing the warm glimmer in his return stare. It was the same one that she'd seen the night of the auction. The light of love. "Well, looks like the crowd still loves you," she said.

Chase smiled and pulled her into his arms. He corrected her, the warmth in his eyes increasing. "I think they're cheering for you," he said.

She laughed again. She couldn't help it. She must've sounded like a fool, but she didn't care. He was back, her second chance, and who, in the real world, ever got two chances at the dream of a lifetime? *Two* chances. It looked like they did.

Chase leaned forward, Jess went up onto her toes, and their lips met.

The fans went wild with applause. Everyone rose to their feet. The cheering grew even louder. Mason and Lindy grinned and clapped. Even Brett, Nina, and Cal were standing, hollering and cheering.

Wesley ran toward his mother and collided with the tangle of Jess and Chase, his arms wrapping around the two of them. Jessica and Chase broke their kiss, and Chase bundled the boy up in his arms, lifting him from the ground.

Even the umpire and the opposing team applauded as Lindy and Mason ran onto the field, followed closely by Brett, Nina, and Cal. Soon, the stands emptied as all of Parker Falls—or so it seemed to Jess—joined Jessica and Chase on the field. Chase had barely let Wes down before Lindy made it to them. She embraced Jess, Mason pulled Chase into a proud bear hug, and Nina barely waited until Jess was free to tackle her best friend.

Jess thought that Chase would be embarrassed that they were surrounded by such a swarm of people, blanketed by rising chatter. But his face was bright, and his smile was wider than the blue Ohio sky. She realized why he was grinning so big.

It's not just how we feel about each other, she thought. *We're surrounded by love.*

Chase found Jess's hand in the fray, and he pulled her back to him. He kissed her sweetly again on the pitcher's mound, to the *ooohs* and *ahhhs* of their entire hometown.

"Welcome home," she whispered when they parted.

"Thanks," Chase replied, "it's good to be home."

Epilogue

*J*ESS TAPED ONE LAST BALLOON to the front display counter, smiling as she looked around at the rest of the decorations covering the dining room. *We might have gone overboard with the streamers.* The banner that hung over the wine display read, "Good Luck Nina and Brett!" and Jess put her hand over the twinge of sadness that pricked at her heart. Nina had been part of Jess's life for so long that Jess wasn't sure what she would do without her bubbly friend.

As if on cue, Nina came bustling out of the kitchen, her arms laden with glittery pink material.

"What is *that*?" Jess asked.

"*These* are tablecloths. They were left over from my cousin's baby shower, but I think they'll work here. I mean, there's glitter, come on."

Jess felt a laugh well up and ease her bittersweet mood. She pictured stoic Brett sitting at a table covered in a glittery pink tablecloth, grinning at Nina with a spark in his eyes. They made an unexpected—but great—pair.

"I think you're right," Jess agreed. She swiped at her

eyes, clearing away the mistiness that clouded them.

Nina set aside the towering stack of tablecloths and grasped Jess's hands. "Hey, are you okay? You're not upset about the move, are you?"

Jess squeezed Nina's hands, reassuring her. "No, no! Not at all. I'm happy you're following your dreams. Beauty school in the city seems so perfect for you. And Brett's new regional position seems right, too. Just think of all the liability in the city!"

Both women laughed. Nina pulled Jess into a hug.

"You inspired both of us to take a chance," Nina said, her own voice wavering slightly. She pulled back from Jess. "And I'll be just as lost without you. But I'll come home. My folks are here, you, Chase, the kids, the diner. My family is in Parker Falls."

A quiet rustling drew Jess's attention. Peering behind the front counter, she checked on the baby, who dozed in her playpen. Jess smiled softly down at the sleeping girl. With Jess's fair skin and Chase's hair color, Jess and Chase's new addition, Ruth, reminded Jess of all the reasons she was glad they'd reunited—and reminded her of Chase's obsession with baseball. She liked to focus on her own traditional inspiration for their daughter's name, ignoring just a little the fact that her husband had liked it for hearkening back to Babe Ruth.

The bell over the front door of the diner chimed. Nina and Jess looked over. Brett came in, followed by Charlie. The two were deep in conversation.

"So, you see," Brett said to the older man, his voice serious, "weevils really are quite a threat to the agriculture out here. Not so much in the city, though. I don't think the weevil clause exists for those contracts."

Charlie looked bewildered and a little bulldozed. "Hey,

ladies," he said, his expression pleading for rescue. Brett opened his mouth to continue, but Nina swooped over with the stack of tablecloths and interrupted before Brett could launch into anymore insurance-speak.

"Honey, no one thinks weevil clauses are interesting." She plopped the tablecloths into Brett's arms. "Here. Come help me put these out."

Brett snapped his mouth closed, and smiled sheepishly. "Hi, Jess," he said, leaning over the stack of sparkling pink to kiss Jess on the cheek. As Brett followed Nina into the dining room, Charlie blew out a breath.

"Thanks," Charlie said, shoving his hands in his pockets. "That guy really likes insurance."

Jess watched Brett follow Nina from table to table, his expression lovestruck. Jess grinned. Insurance wasn't the only thing Brett was enamored of.

Turning back to Charlie, she said, "So, you ready for the food truck festival Saturday? I've got my truck all stocked up. We're expecting a big crowd."

Charlie nodded. "Just got 'er back from Mason's. She's all tuned up and ready to go. I think upscale-on-wheels is really going to be successful. And, hey, Emberto's Tacos registered their truck for the festival last-minute, so I think we're up to a dozen trucks now."

"From three counties!" Jess added. "The Spring Fling committee was happy with the extra sponsorship. Adding the food truck festival to the last weekend couldn't have worked out better. We did good."

Charlie nodded. "Yeah, we did. You tell that husband of yours that I expect to see you both on Sunday night for dinner at my restaurant. Candlelight, crab, and crème brûlée. On the house. Get a sitter!"

Jess nodded, stifling more laughter at the gruff restaurateur who'd quickly become a friend. "You got it, Charlie." Charlie moved to help Nina and Brett, and Jess looked down at her left hand and the modest diamond sparkling on it. *Husband.* Even a year later, it still seemed too good to be true. Like a fairy tale.

The bell chimed over the door again, and Chase and Wes came barreling in, followed by Mason and Lindy. Chase and Wes were chattering excitedly, and Lindy shushed them.

"Shhhh, boys! The baby might be sleeping," Lindy admonished. Chase blanched, and Wes put his hands over his mouth. Ruth began to fuss. The group made its way to Jess, who bustled behind the counter and scooped Ruth up, bringing her back out to be kissed and cooed over by her grandparents.

Cal came out of the kitchen with a steaming buffet dish, and Lindy and Mason moved to help him bring out the rest of the food.

Chase put an arm around Jess and drew the baby and her closer. He mussed Wes's hair. "You'd have been so proud of Wes today. He was a real help at spring training. I didn't know he could spot range or speed like such a pro."

Wes lifted his beaming face toward Jess. "Mom, Mom, seriously, it was the best. I was right behind home plate! All the players talked to me!"

Jess squeezed Wes with her free arm, and she smiled widely at Chase. Chase's answering smile made her heart flutter. The love that filled his eyes was a direct reflection of the love that filled her heart. He leaned in and placed a soft kiss on her cheek.

"Hey," he said.

"Hi," she said back.

Wes disentangled from his parents and ran over to Nina, Brett, and Charlie, who were now setting up a punchbowl. Chase nudged Jess.

"Here, I'll take her," Chase offered, and Jess slid Ruth over to her father, who cradled her close and looked down at the baby with the same awe on his face that Jess felt every day.

"The place looks great. You guys did a lot of work. Why don't you go relax for a few minutes?" Chase said. Jess took another look around the diner, reaching out a hand to wipe an invisible smudge off of the display case full of sweets. The display didn't spin anymore, but she didn't need it to distract her. Her life had come a full, perfect circle.

"Nah," she said to Chase. "I'll stay out here"—she linked one of her hands with one of his—"with my family."

The End

Bacon & White Cheddar Burgers with Spicy Mustard Relish

A Hallmark Original Recipe

In *The Perfect Catch*, Chase helps Jess with her food truck and "autographs" one of the burgers with mustard. Jess puts a creative spin on diner food, just like this recipe does. It'll take your burger game to a whole new level.

Yield: 4 Burgers
Prep Time: 15 minutes
Cook Time: 15 minutes

INGREDIENTS

Spicy Mustard Relish:

- ¼ cup pickle relish
- 2 tablespoons yellow mustard
- 2 tablespoons ketchup
- ½ teaspoon sriracha sauce (adjust quantity based on your preference)

- 1¾ pounds ground beef chuck
- Salt and freshly ground black pepper
- 4 slices sharp white Cheddar cheese
- 4 brioche hamburger buns, buttered and toasted
- ¼ cup mayonnaise
- ¼ head iceberg lettuce, shredded
- ¼ cup thin-sliced red onion
- 8 bacon slices, cooked crisp

DIRECTIONS

1. To prepare relish: Combine pickle relish, mustard, ketchup and sriracha sauce in a small bowl and stir to blend; reserve.
2. Shape ground beef into four 5-inch round patties; season to taste with salt and black pepper. Heat a heavy cast iron pan or griddle over medium heat. Add patties and cook on each side for 5 minutes, or until cooked to desired doneness. Top each burger with a slice of cheese and heat briefly to melt cheese.
3. To assemble burgers: spread 1 tablespoon mayonnaise on bottom half of each bun; top each evenly with shredded lettuce, red onion, white Cheddar burgers, crispy bacon slices and spicy mustard relish. Close with top halves of buns.
4. Optional: To "autograph" your plate, use a

mustard squeeze bottle and shake it well, so it is thoroughly mixed. Making sure the top cap is turned where it will not interfere with the flow of the mustard, hold it about two inches away from the plate. In one continuous loop, using cursive, write the name of a child or an encouraging word!

Thanks so much for reading
The Perfect Catch. We hope you enjoyed it!

You might like these other books from Hallmark
Publishing:

Journey Back to Christmas
Christmas in Homestead
Love You Like Christmas
A Heavenly Christmas
A Dash of Love
Moonlight in Vermont
Love Locks

For information about our new releases and exclusive offers, sign up for our free newsletter at
hallmarkchannel.com/hallmark-publishing-newsletter

You can also connect with us here:

Facebook.com/HallmarkPublishing

Twitter.com/HallmarkPublish